CHORE
WARS

CHORE WARS

How Households
can **SHARE**
the work
&
keep the
PEACE

JAMES THORNTON

Foreword by Marcia Lasswell, president of
the American Association for Marriage and Family Therapy

CONARI PRESS
Berkeley, CA

Conari Press books are distributed by Publishers Group West

ISBN: 1-57324-054-0

Cover design by Suzanne Albertson

Library of Congress Cataloging-in-Publication Data
Thorton, James, 1952–
        Chore wars: how households can share the work & keep the peace /
James Thornton.
            p.   cm.
        ISBN 1-57324-054-0 (trade paper)
        1. House cleaning.   2. Home economics.   I. Title.
    TX324.T5   1997   96-52839
    648'.5—dc21

Printed in the United States of America on recycled paper
10 9 8 6 5 4 3 2 1

For my mother, Elizabeth,

my sister, Liza,

and my wife, Debbie

CONTENTS

FOREWORD

As both a therapist and a psychology professor specializing in marriage and family therapy, I recognize the problems presented in *Chore Wars* as common causes for unhappiness in modern relationships. With its array of non-blaming, pragmatic solutions, I'm sure *Chore Wars* will not only make an enduring contribution as a self-help book, I also believe therapists will want to recommend it to clients grappling with these issues.

Mr. Thornton's book is also just plain fun to read with its "war stories" from dozens of households, stories that are by turns funny, infuriating, and poignant. He also charts his own evolution from "the kind of husband that has caused so much sociological hand-wringing" to a fully contributing—and much happier—member of his own household.

The book provides great advice, too, on the domestic arts. I thought I knew just about everything there was to know about cleaning and feeding a family after having done this for four decades. But *Chore Wars* taught me a few new tricks. For instance, when the author realized how inadequate his own cleaning skills were, he decided to hire a professional housecleaner—not to do the jobs, but to teach him how to do them. What a great idea! This is just one of the many revelations from *Chore Wars* that I will definitely be recommending to my own clients.

On a personal note, very soon my granddaughter will be going off to college where she's arranged to live with three new housemates. I'm sure they will all profit from reading *Chore Wars*, so I'll be sending a copy along in a "care package" in the near future. Ditto for her parents—they've been married a long time now, but they continue to struggle in their dual-career marriage with who does what around the house. When I told them about this wonderful new book, they let me know they wanted their copy ASAP.

In short, I'm convinced this book will be of tremendous benefit to anyone whose home life suffers from an unfair division of labor (which is to say, most of us!).

—Marcia Lasswell, M.A., President of the American Association for Marriage and Family Therapy; professor of marriage and family therapy at the University of Southern California; and professor of psychology at California State University in Pomona.

Chapter 1

RESTORING DOMESTIC TRANQUILITY

Why Sharing Home Work Will Make Your Life *Better*

Every man is dishonest who lives upon the labor of others,
no matter if he occupies a throne.
> —Robert Green Ingersoll

Marriage is that relation between man and woman
in which the independence is equal, the dependence mutual,
and the obligation reciprocal.
> —Louis K. Anspacher

It takes two to make a marriage a success
and only one to make it a failure.
> —Herbert Samuel

A person's politics really have a lot less to do with whether
they'd make a good roommate than do their day-to-day habits
around the house. If cleanliness is important to you, you're
probably going to be lot happier living with a neat anarchist
than a messy law-and-order fanatic.
> —Shelly D.

In the eighth month of pregnancy with our second child, my wife was diagnosed with high blood pressure and ordered to total bed rest by her doctor. I had always been the sort of husband who "helped" with housework, that is, if I had the time and Debbie told me exactly what to do. But suddenly, I found myself 100 percent in charge of everything on the homefront—from laundry and house cleaning to getting our four-year-old son, Ben, dressed each morning and cooking food he would actually consider eating.

It took me about five minutes of full-time house husbandry to realize how much work my wife had been shouldering for years. It took me even less time to realize how truly pathetic I was in terms of domestic competence. How exactly *do* you cook macaroni and cheese? What button do you push to make the washing machine go—and what about that weird dial with all those settings? Why are these dust bunnies beading up when I wash them with a wet rag?

The comedy of such helpless malehood aside, the truth was I felt genuinely ashamed of myself. All of a sudden, my family really *needed* me to run our household, and my years of abdicating all these responsibilities to Debbie had left me without a clue.

To her everlasting credit, Debbie did not shower upon me the castigation I knew I deserved. Instead, she suggested I grab a little notebook to jot down her answers to my numerous questions about housework. Over the next few weeks, this notebook became my ever constant companion, the information inside it growing daily. From her bed, Debbie patiently provided directions for all our household gadgets, from the programmable oven to the terrifying steam iron. She gave me advice on operating low-tech gizmos, as well, from the mop to the squeegee. She instructed me on cooking techniques and basic recipes: frying bacon so it's cooked but not charred, for instance, and giving rice flavor by steaming it in chicken broth.

With her help, I also compiled a master shopping list of food staples. And then, because it drove me crazy to hunt for items in the grocery store, I marked down on my list the aisle number where each item can be found.

In another section of my notebook, I jotted down a list of phone numbers for take-out food and pizza delivery; babysitters; pediatricians and the poison center; and Ben's friends and directions to their homes. I also put together a day-by-day list of chores so I could wake up and—without having to think about it—simply look and see what I need to get done that day.

This chores-by-number approach might sound comical to people who have a kind of chores Dayrunner ingrained in their synapses, but for me it was tremendously helpful to have, written down in one place, "how" and "when" instructions for every task I needed to do.

Amazingly, it worked—and in a much grander way than I could have imagined possible. My little notebook, I now see in retrospect, was only the practical manifestation of a deeper emotional change that, once initiated, has continued to evolve over the years. Without consciously realizing it at the time, Debbie and I had begun—slowly, surely, and for the most part without rancor—to reconfigure our relationship not only to domestic work but to each other as well. It turns out that sharing responsibilities made us both happier—Debbie because she was no longer burdened by a disproportionate set of the tasks, and me because her happiness had a positive domino effect on the whole family.

Debbie's stint of bed rest ended up helping more than just our marriage blossom. About a month later, she went into the one kind of domestic labor I will never be able to share. The result was our second child, Jack, a healthy baby boy. Debbie, whose blood pressure returned to normal within minutes of Jack's birth, is fine and back to work at home. But she is no longer shouldering the housework all by herself.

I am taking a share, too. And so is Ben—admittedly, a rather little one, but one both Debbie and I are dedicated to seeing grow over the years. After all, Ben and I are now masculine role models for little Jack who, even as we speak, is drooling a fine spit-polish sheen onto the dining room table.

A Journey Worth Taking

I don't mean to gloss over the difficulties we've had making—and maintaining—these changes. But through my own family's hard-won successes, along with those I've witnessed in scores of other families, I've come to see that the chore wars truly can be ended—and once ended, your household can reap a peace dividend that's hard to imagine during the throes of bitterness.

If we can do it, I am convinced you can, too. It's not always easy, but the effort is well worth it. As Henry Ford once put it, "Coming together is a beginning; keeping together is progress; working together is success."

To be sure, coming together—in the sense of sharing a unified vision on how to run a household—is not a simple matter. The truth is, most contemporary men and women carry a lot of baggage when it comes to how, and who, should run a household. My own background, I suspect, is more the manly rule than the exception. I spent a fifties-era childhood growing up in a Pittsburgh suburb. My father worked long hours at a spring manufacturing company; my mother stayed at home with me, my identical twin brother, John, and our younger sister, Lizie. Our mother did everything for us—cooking, cleaning, bed-making, clothes-shopping, doctor-toting, station wagon–chauffeuring, and the innumerable other unsung duties of the traditional housewife. When Lizie was old enough to help out, she was encouraged to do so. For my brother and me, it was a different story: Once in a blue moon we'd be ordered to make our beds or mow the grass. But for the most part, we were allowed to grow up like perfect *enfants sauvages*, altogether undisturbed by domestic demands.

This continued into our college years. Home for vacation, I'd wake to my mother's fine cooked breakfast (a stark contrast to the coffee and aspirin I'd usually "cook" for myself). By the time I'd finished eating and ascended back upstairs to take a shower, my bed was always made. And by the time I'd finished my shower and descended back downstairs to watch a rerun of *The Beverly Hillbillies,* my breakfast dishes were washed and put away.

Ditto for the underwear, socks, and T-shirt I'd left lying on the floor by the shower.

Ditto for every crumb and smudge that followed me, like the tail of a comet, in my progress through the day.

When I left home for good, I had no idea how to run the dishwasher, the washing machine, or the dryer, or how to use an iron—I was technologically illiterate on the homefront. Worse, I didn't know how to sweep or mop; even household low-tech was beyond me. Over the subsequent decade and a half of bachelorhood, I eventually did pick up enough domestic skills to sort of get by.

I learned, for instance, how to grill meat and cook boil-in-the-bag frozen vegetables. Trial and error taught me the folly of washing a month-long accumulation of dirty laundry—from gym socks to Oxford shirts—in one monster Laundromat load. Indeed, by the time Debbie and I met in graduate school, I'd created for myself a degree of domestic civilization that probably surpassed by some slight measure that described in William Golding's classic story of young men on their own, *Lord of the Flies.*

But when Debbie and I got married in 1983, there was never any question in either of our minds that a house with her stamp on it was likely to be superior to one with my stamp on it. I quickly assumed the role of helper. Because my job as a freelance journalist called for more hours than her job running a home-based pearl button company, it was easy for me to rationalize my shortcomings on an ever growing number of occasions when my help was late in coming, or perhaps never came at all. Debbie, who, like me, was raised in a home where girls were expected to shoulder more housework than boys, tried reminding me, and, when this in itself became a chore, she went ahead and eventually took up any slack I provided her with.

She wasn't happy about this state of affairs, of course, though she rarely lost her temper with me. More common was a kind of chronic low-grade irritation that sometimes seemed to me to drain all the fun out of our marriage. I didn't always equate this irritation with Debbie's being overworked—in fact, I tried to chalk it up to other factors: hormones, cold viruses, a bad night's sleep, and various other usual suspects. Still, somewhere in the back of my mind, I realized I was treating Debbie like an unpaid servant. I felt guilty—but not guilty enough to change. And the truth was I was paying dearly.

And so it was that without conscious effort on either of our parts, our marriage inevitably began to recapitulate the gender roles we'd both grown up with, but in a time when such roles no longer reflected contemporary economic realities. The American male's life cycle, at least in my case and that of most of my friends, resembled something out of zoology—a juvenile phase during which we are cared for by our moth-ers; a short free-swimming interlude where we semicare for ourselves; and a mature phase where we once again resume our place being cared for by females we love.

There Must Be Some Way Out of Here

In one of life's little ironies, this whole topic of housework and its impact on working spouses was one in which I had taken a keen pro-fessional interest long before Debbie's mandated bed rest jolted me into taking the issue personally. Several different national magazines had assigned me to write stories on different aspects of what was then—and still is—an overwhelmingly inequitable division of household labor between men and women.

Earlier that same year, I interviewed dozens of two-career couples across the country, along with researchers and psychologists from insti-tutions such as the University of California at Berkeley, the Wellesley College Center for Research on Women, New York University, the American Association for Marriage and Family Therapy, and the Menninger Clinic in Topeka, Kansas.

In the process, I came to recognize that this issue, which so many men in their heart of hearts try to shrug off as trivial, is anything but. Indeed, back in the early eighties, University of California at Berkeley sociologist Arlie Hochschild wrote a landmark book on the subject, which she entitled *The Second Shift: Working Parents and the Revolution at Home.* "Second shift" remains a phrase that working women every-where still use as a shorthand description for the additional solo labor that awaits so many of them when they return home from their day jobs.

In the two-career couples Hochschild surveyed, she found that women over the course of a year work on average an extra month of twenty-four-hour days. Over the course of a dozen years, women work an extra year of twenty-four-hour days. Hochschild does a superb job documenting the social and political components of what seems to many couples a private, personal source of unhappiness.

In writing this solutions-oriented book, I've gleaned a smorgasbord of additional statistics from a wide array of researchers and other sources. Not all of these are dry and academic. For instance, how do you think the average husband would think the average wife would answer the following questions?

- Would you prefer an evening of lovemaking or a perfectly clean house?

- Would you rather have okay sex in a clean house or great sex in a dirty house?

- Would you rather marry a man who looks like Robert Redford but does no chores, or a man who looks like Danny DeVito but does half the chores?

You'll find the answer to the Redford/DeVito question and other pressing concerns in an amusing chore wars poll at the end of this chapter. First take a moment to consider a few other statistics a bit less likely to provoke a laugh. I have divided these stats into several categories for easy reference:

Category 1: Damn Us Men!

- 56 percent of married American men have wives who work outside the home. Some studies have shown that these women do 70 percent of the housework (as compared to the 83 percent share undertaken by full-time homemakers).

- Two independent university studies indicate that for most guys, it doesn't seem to matter whether their wives work outside the home or not—men tend to do the same, minimal amount of work regardless of wifely employment status.

- Single mothers spend an average of sixteen hours a week on chores versus twenty hours for married mothers. This has led some researchers to speculate that the main household contribution of many husbands is more mess.

- Even in countries where it's illegal for husbands to shirk their home duties, men apparently feel more comfortable as scofflaws than helpmates. In Cuba, for instance, husbands are legally mandated to share chores with their wives—and yet 80 percent of housework is still done by the women.

- Generational changes in attitudes are occurring, but the pace is glacial. In a survey of male seniors at the University of California at Berkeley (it's hard to imagine you could find a more politically correct sample group), only 31 percent said they expected to share cooking duties with their female partners. Fully twice as many of Berkeley's female seniors, on the other hand, said they expected egalitarianism in the kitchen.

- Robin A. Douthitt of the University of Wisconsin at Madison's Institute for Research on Poverty has proposed a novel way at looking at the overload faced by so many women. Just as economic poverty has a ruinous effect on quality of life, so does the time poverty endured by so many working women. Indeed, one researcher observed: "These women talk about sleep the way a hungry person talks about food."

- Men, on average, tend to earn more than their wives—a fact that "big paycheck" guys use to justify a hands-off approach to household management. Averages can be misleading, however. The New York–based, non-profit Families and Work Institute randomly surveyed 1,502 women and 460 men and found that 55 percent of working women actually brought in half or more of their family's household income.

- Even in couples where the wife earns nothing, her contributions are substantial in purely economic terms. In the early 1980s, family practice attorney Michael Harry Minton, coauthor of *What Is a Life Worth?*, listed all the main job duties of the typical homemaker and the average hours per week performed on each one. He then tallied up the cost of hiring a full-time homemaker. To update Minton's figures to reflects today's wages, the Washington, D.C.–based association, Women Work! The National Network for Women's Employment, factored in the most recent U.S. Department of Labor wage rates. Here's their tally:

Job Performed	Hours per week	Rate/hour	Value/week
Food Buyer	3.00	12.02	36.06
Nurse	1.00	15.72	15.72
Tutor	2.00	14.01	28.02
Waitress	2.25	5.77	12.98
Seamstress	75.00	8.87	6.63
Laundress	3.00	3.21	9.63
Chauffeur	3.50	8.75	30.63
Gardener	2.25	7.27	16.36
Family Counselor	2.00	92.00	184.00
Maintenance Worker	1.00	7.46	7.46
Nanny	40.00	3.75	150.07
Cleaning Woman	7.50	4.95	37.13
Housekeeper	2.50	4.81	12.03
Cook	12.00	6.67	80.04
Errand Runner	3.50	9.25	32.38
Bookkeeper/Budget Manager	3.50	9.03	31.61
Interior Decorator	1.00	32.00	32.00
Caterer	1.50	11.54	17.31
Child Psychologist	5.00	92.00	460.00
Household Buyer	2.00	14.18	28.36
Dishwasher	6.20	5.66	35.09
Dietitian	1.20	11.38	13.66
Secretary	2.00	9.21	18.42
Public Relations/Hostess	1.00	15.84	15.84

Bottom line: Weekly Value—$1,311.45

Yearly Value—$68,195.40

Clearly, it would take a pretty substantial salary gap to make a dent in this figure—despite the fact that homemaking remains in reality the indisputably lowest paid job in America. Most homemakers get paid nothing at all.

Category 2: Praise Us Men!

- On the plus side, American men aren't the world's worst. A University of Connecticut regional study indicates we spend an average of 108 minutes a day on chores and child care—as opposed to eleven minutes per day spent by Japanese men.

- Also on the plus side, researcher Joseph Pleck, Ph.D., Luce Professor of Families, Change, and Society at Wheaton College in Massachusetts, has found that, at least when it comes to child rearing, today's generation of dads spend significantly more time with their kids than their own fathers spent with them. It's still not fifty-fifty but the trend is clearly encouraging. (Two caveats: men still tend to select more of the fun stuff—like taking their kids to the zoo. And women, by and large, are still ultimately responsible for the kids, with men playing a supporting role as helpers.)

- Demographer John P. Robinson of the University of Maryland has conducted extensive time use surveys, and his data also argue that some positive change has already occurred in both sexes—and more positive change is likely to be forthcoming. From 1965 to 1985, Robinson found, women reduced the time spent on cooking, cleaning, and laundry by an average of eight hours a week. Men, on the other hand, have shown themselves to be doing an ever greater share of these over the past three decades. Consider: Men during the Summer of Love era averaged only 15 percent of the total housework load. But by the time of Ronald Reagan's inauguration, this figure had climbed to 33 percent.

- In a major 1996 study sponsored by the National Institute of Mental Health, Rosalind C. Barnett, Ph.D., of the Murray Research Center at Radcliffe College, found the housework gap continues to narrow—with working men's share up to 45 percent compared to 55 percent by working women. Women still shoulder more responsibility for very young children, but, by the time the kids reach school age, parenting hours are nearly equal.

- Perhaps the most interesting proof that this trend toward "collaborative couples" is real is the fact that advertisers have begun to take men seriously as household workers, with companies like Black & Decker pitching household products specifically to men. It may only be a matter of time before a Johnny Homemaker toy line hits your local toy store.

Category 3: What Exactly Do Women Want?

- Complicating all this is that women themselves often send mixed messages about what kinds of change they would like to see their men make. One anthropologist found that men and women derive different benefits and rewards from a well-maintained home.

Women, much more than men, tend to derive greater satisfaction and improved self-image from a job done right.

- In a survey of working women, 53 percent candidly conceded that they don't want to give up any responsibilities either at home or at work. This sentiment was even stronger in younger individuals. 60 percent of women aged eighteen to thirty-four said they wouldn't want to give up either role versus 56 percent of women aged thirty-five to forty-four, and 48 percent of those between forty-five and fifty-five.

- It's a myth that lots of women would secretly like to return to the hearth. When asked if they would continue working even if money were not a consideration, 48 percent of working women said yes—compared to 61 percent of men.

- Despite this, the women in the survey cited lack of time as their single most pressing concern—ranking it above issues of both crime and safety.

Ignorance Is Hardly Bliss

OK, OK. I admit that the lion's share of these statistics is not exactly flattering to my gender, even if a few of them might be at least borderline exculpatory. To be sure, there's no single male response to the most damning of these domestic data. For a handful of guys who acknowledge the blatant unfairness, realization alone appears to provide sufficient motivation to change. According to social psychologist Joseph Pleck, one out of ten American couples do share household duties equally.

There are even cases where working men undertake all the household work. "Because of a chronic neuromuscular illness I suffer," says a former cosmetics company executive in California, "my husband does pretty much everything around our house. I suspect most wives find themselves in the opposite situation, but I know at least one great guy who's really been a household saint."

The occasional counterexample notwithstanding, household saint is not exactly a moniker that fits the great unwashed majority of us

American males. Instead, most of us choose to pretty much ignore the inequitable division of labor factoids.

But we ignore them at our own peril. Make no mistake: Overworked women are increasingly miserable—and increasingly willing to share this misery with the men they love. In a recent Roper poll, more than half of all married women reported resenting their husbands for not doing more housework. In some cases, this resentment festers to the point of divorce.

As anyone—man or woman—who has lived with an actively resentful partner knows all too well, there are times you'd be happier married to a wolverine. The truth is, one way or another, you're likely to get bitten. Recalls Arlie Hochschild about the couples she studied where men either refused outright or acted in a passive-aggressive manner to avoid household work: "I came to realize that those husbands who helped very little at home were often just as deeply affected as their wives—through the resentment their wives felt toward them and through their own needs to steel themselves against that resentment."

Uxorial revenge can also hit below the belt. Hochschild remembers the case of a furniture salesman who did very little housework and played with the couple's four-year-old son only at his convenience. His wife keenly resented having to shoulder the second shift alone. Recalls Hochschild: "Half-consciously, she expressed her frustration and rage by losing interest in sex and becoming overly absorbed in their son."

It could be worse, especially for guys who want to stay married. In a study of 600 couples filing for divorce, researcher George Levinger found that "neglect of home or children" was second only to "mental cruelty" as the most frequently cited grounds for breaking up.

The more couples I interviewed, the more clearly I began to realize how huge a problem chore wars really are. Indeed, every marriage therapist I interviewed reiterated the point: Fights over housework were one of the single most common, though often uncredited, causes for strife and unhappiness between couples and between parents and children.

Whether the chore wars lead to a dismal sex life, incessant battles with older children, or simply a chronic drone of discord to the music of your household, the truth is that no one wins when a situation becomes blatantly one-sided and unfair.

Why This Book

After the first of my articles appeared in print, I was astonished by how big a nerve it struck with readers. The magazine received an outpouring of letters from women nationwide whose marriages were suffering because of their husbands' lack of contribution at home. The article was eventually syndicated in newspapers across the country, and I found myself fielding calls from national TV talk show producers anxious to interview the couples I'd profiled—and to offer their viewers sound-bite solutions to this incredibly complex problem.

All this, of course, left me more than a little taken aback. Over the course of my career, I'd written about a wide spectrum of topics, from sled-dog poodle mushing to the evolution of male philandering. But never had any of my stories come close to triggering such a response.

I found myself asked over and over to recommend a single, one-stop book expressly dedicated to providing practical solutions to chore wars. At first, I just assumed there must be a surfeit of self-help volumes on the subject. Surely for such a common problem, someone must have perceived a need and written a guide to the psychological and behavioral changes necessary to reach a truce. My own preliminary research convinced me there was plenty of extremely useful information out there in the research literature, not to mention in the minds of psychologists, therapists, and individuals themselves. But when I started to look for a book that brought all this wisdom together in one place and in pragmatic, layman's language, I found, to my surprise, that none existed.

The bottom line, I realized, was that couples with marriages on the verge of foundering because of chore wars might find answers if they were lucky enough to find a good therapist. But the lion's share of us, who could really benefit from some good self-help solutions, were on our own and out of luck. It was to fill this need that I dedicated myself to writing *Chore Wars*.

If you're reading this book now, odds are pretty good that you're the overworked member of the household—in all likelihood, a woman whose husband (and perhaps you yourself) considers the second shift mostly, if not entirely, your responsibility. You may well have already tried and failed to make things fairer, and you're probably feeling more than a little bit desperate that nothing will ever change.

A smaller percentage of you readers are likely to be husbands suffering your own form of unhappiness—the kind that echoes back to you from the exhaustion and resentment of your wife. Perhaps your wife has thrust this book upon you, demanding you read it. Perhaps you see that your relationship is in jeopardy, and you've picked up a copy in the hopes of saving your marriage. You, too, probably feel some desperation, sense that the two of you are stuck and that you will never stop feeling bad about this issue.

Take heart: This book can set you both on the road to a new and happier life. These techniques really worked in my own family, and they've helped countless others across the nation to change as well. At the risk of repeating myself, know this: You can end the chore wars and restore harmony to your relationship.

Help for Housemates, Too

Of course, you don't have to be a median American family with 2.2 children to live in a household where chore wars can exact a devastating toll. From parents living with adult children, to gay and lesbian couples, to the potpourri of urban adults who find themselves thrown together in a joint household just to afford big city rents, myriad domestic arrangements exist across the country. As different as some of these may seem on the surface from a traditional marriage, the same basic principles usually apply—not to mention the same miseries and the same crying need for solutions.

Take Scott, sixty-one, a French and German teacher at a midwestern high school. For the past twenty-two years, Scott has lived with his friend and fellow teacher, Pinchas, fifty-seven. Besides companionship, the two have derived obvious financial benefits from cohabitation. Together, for example, they can afford a nice house with a pool, something that neither one, on a teacher's salary, could come close to affording alone.

When they first moved in together in 1974, Scott, a gourmet cook, prepared healthy dinners each night. Pinchas, for his part, pitched in with cleaning and house maintenance. But over the years, Scott found himself in charge of more and more of the domestic jobs—and Pinchas was content to sit back and let his friend take up the slack. Without quite realizing how it happened, Scott woke up one day to find himself in charge of virtually everything domestic: housecleaning, shopping, cooking, gardening, pool maintenance, bill-paying, and entertaining. There were only two significant exceptions: Pinchas paid someone to cut the grass. And when he was unable to convince Scott to do his laundry, Pinchas found someone else to do it—his eighty-year-old mother.

As the years passed, Scott found himself more and more resentful over this imbalance, though he kept his feelings to himself. "Each of us is a very independent person," he says. "We both tend to internalize our feelings to avoid rocking the boat." Now, as the two old friends appear likely to dissolve their household and live alone for the first time in more than two decades, Scott finds himself regretting the fact that they ever let things get so far out of balance. "I really think in retrospect that discussion and the exchange of ideas is critical," he says. "I wish we would have ritualized something like this—decided, for instance, that each month we would set aside one hour to talk about how things were going in the household."

Housemate Horrors

For roommates who don't even have the bonds of mutual affection to motivate some sort of chore wars accord, unfairness in domestic duties can become the single greatest degrader of the quality of life. Take, for example, the following roommate horror story lived out by Brenda, a young female marketing manager who moved to San Francisco in 1984.

"I had just graduated from college," she says, "and I was moving from the small town of Gallipolis in southeast Ohio, where everyone kept their houses and yards in impeccable shape. There, you could rent an entire floor of a large house for $200 a month. When I reached San Francisco, I was shocked to find that $200 literally wouldn't get you a closet. I very quickly realized that the only way I could afford to live in this city was to find roommates. A friend told me about a roommate referral service, something that I have since learned exists in all major urban centers."

When Brenda arrived at the roommate referral office, she was given lists and lists of rooms that were available, livable, and affordable. Brenda found it particularly amusing how different households advertised for just the right person to fit in with their collective temperaments. It was not unusual, for instance, to read a phrase like: "Looking for bisexual, vegetarian, non-smoking Wiccan with a minimum of four tattoos." But as comically specific as these descriptions could be, very few of them mentioned anything about a person's housekeeping standards—and then only in vague terms like "Looking for someone reasonably responsible."

Before long, Brenda had located a house that seemed very promising—a huge Queen Anne Victorian not far from the intersection of Haight and Ashbury made so famous during the psychedelic era. As she walked up the pathway to be interviewed by the existing residents, she noticed that the exterior hadn't been painted for years. Still, the romance of the architecture captured her imagination, and she found herself really hoping that the roommates would accept her into the fold.

They were certainly amiable enough, two young men and two young women, all fresh out of college, too. They asked her what kind of music she liked to listen to, what kinds of books she read, what her college major was. By the end of the interview, Brenda liked them—and they liked her. She was in.

Only then did she notice that the place was a little decrepit inside as well as out. Though the roommates had evidently tried to straighten things up—it was in their interest, after all, to attract a new renter to help subsidize their own share—the common living spaces were, frankly, disheveled and dirty. Beer cans, week-old newspapers, pizza boxes: The place seemed to smack ever so slightly of unregulated dorm life.

Not too worry, Brenda told herself—a little fresh paint, some lemon oil rubbed into the natural woodwork, flowers in the living room: All the place needed was a few tidying touches to restore its lost elegance. As she moved her belongings in a week later, all seemed more or less right with her world—just as the opening chapter of a Stephen King novel usually gives only vague hints of the creep show to come.

In Brenda's case, she didn't need to wait long. Within a week of her moving in, one of her male roommates started a punk band, and the house immediately became the band's favorite hangout—a place to chain smoke and drink beer till the whole house was overflowing with ashes and crushed aluminum cans. The band, a kind of musical locust plague, had no compunction about eating anything they could scavenge, and they frequently stole Brenda's food, which they munched till the wee hours while watching Brady Bunch reruns.

Then one of her female roommates left town without telling anyone, and a few days later, the woman's cat gave birth to a litter of kittens. These cute little fur balls quickly grew into feral beasts that destroyed the rugs and scratched up all the furniture. The cat's owner never did return—leaving the remaining roommates to cover the cost of the damages.

To make things worse, the Victorian architecture that had once seemed so romantic to Brenda quickly proved why servants were so popular, and necessary, in the Victorian era. The house was riddled with odd nooks and crannies that were magnets for dust bunnies and live vermin. An odd series of abandoned conduits—former laundry chutes?—seemed to whisk and swirl dinginess from one drafty corner of the house to the other. Perhaps most shocking of all was something Brenda found growing in between the bathroom tiles one morning after the season had turned cold, gray, and rainy. Mushrooms—slender and wispy like Shiitakes: The bathroom was like a farm for fungus.

It was around this time when Brenda learned that one of her remaining female housemates had herself tried to restore some sort of order to the house, only to give up and surrender to the gloom. After a month of valiant effort, Brenda, too, gave up. "My midwestern optimism," she says today, "really got a reality check. I learned that the simple values I grew up with are not universal by any means. People can have real different ideas of how to live, and some of these ideas are kind of scary."

After six months, Brenda couldn't stand it anymore, and she moved out, convinced that she'd escaped the worst household imaginable. She was wrong. One of her friends later related an even worse episode. The friend had needed a roommate and had eventually agreed to share her quarters with a woman teacher. Within several weeks of moving in, the teacher installed locks on both the outside and inside of her room. Soon, she became virtually invisible, hiding inside her room for days on end. She stopped paying rent and eventually had to be evicted. When the authorities finally unlocked the room, they found rotting food everywhere interspersed with bottles of urine.

Telling Stories: A Brief Overview

In the three years it has taken me to write this book, I have collected literally hundreds of chore war stories from the lives of working couples and housemates. Though only one of these, thank god, involved rotting meat and urine, all of the men and women I interviewed nevertheless spoke with great poignancy on this often trivialized aspect of daily life. "People tend to think that relationships succeed or fail because of the big, lofty issues like love, fidelity, and financial security," one fifty-five-year-old woman told me. "But it's not these lofty things that ultimately define a marriage. It's the little, day-to-day, nitty gritty things like housework—the stuff that needs to be done every day—that can really grind you down and steal the love away. I really wish my ex-husband and I could have resolved these issues better, and shared the work more fairly. The nitty gritty stuff is what destroyed our marriage."

Some of the stories in this book I obtained by conducting traditional oral interviews of couples; in other cases, one or both spouses agreed to my request that they write down their innermost feelings about domestic work. My only stipulation was that the latter respondents not confer with their partner during the writing process, though they were free to share their essays with each other afterward. I wanted, as much as possible, to get unbiased reports from the trenches, essays that had not been given any spin-doctoring by a mate hoping to cast himself—or herself—in a better light. Whenever asked, I agreed not to use real names—an anonymity that encouraged further candor.

The responses I received were astonishing—at turns funny and full of fury, optimistic and almost unbearably sad. Sometimes couples appeared to be describing life on different planets. Other times, they were in perfect synchrony, even if this meant they were equally overwhelmed by the workloads they were trying to shoulder.

When I showed some of these responses to a friend, he said, "It's almost as if you can read a whole relationship into these essays. They're like a Rorschach ink blot for the state of these relationships."

I was also amazed by the seriousness with which both men and women discussed the topic of household work. Though many incorporated humor, none took the assignment lightly—in fact, if anything, some people declined to participate out of fear that even thinking about this topic would cause problems in their house. "I won't do it," one lawyer told me flatly, then begged me not to approach his wife, a real estate broker, about my request. "It would just start a fight over a problem we didn't even know we had."

Lawyerly denial notwithstanding, the odds are overwhelming that both mates, on some level, do know a problem exists—and writing it down, I was delighted to discover, can be a great way to start a dialogue that can ultimately be healing and transforming.

As one advertising executive married to a woman who holds public office confessed to me: "Writing my thoughts on this subject was at first enormously depressing. I like to think I'm a decent guy and in no way a sexist. In fact, if you had asked me on the street how my wife and I divide household work, I wouldn't have hesitated to answer that we share chores fifty-fifty. But when I really started to think about it, it hit me like a sledgehammer. She does much more than me, and I am really trying now to make things more fair."

Complex Issues:
When Change Is a Two-Way Street

It may be some small consolation to overworked women that this ad man's guilt was extremely common among almost all the men who admitted taking a backseat on the homefront. Still, despite the apparent one-way culpability, the researchers and couples I interviewed agreed that the inequitable division of household labor is a more complex business than any variation on the reductionist "Her good, him bad" theme can explain. For both spouses, the chore war is a psychodrama with roots reaching deep into gender image, fairness, and balance of power. As family psychologist Gail Hartman told me, "The housework fight is rarely about the task alone. Couples tend to think it is just about who does the dishes. It's not about dishes. It is about intimacy and taking responsibility. It is a problem with many tentacles."

On the other hand, as Nolan Brohaugh, M.S.W., of the Menninger Clinic pointed out, it is also a problem with a very practical component—many men just don't know how to do common chores. Witness a recent episode of *Oprah,* which showed a husband using a Dustbuster to vacuum the greasy burners on the kitchen stove.

Brohaugh, who conducts seminars for executive couples on ways to cope with home and work stresses, says a basic lack of domestic know-how by men is a significant, and often underrated, cause of strife. Cleaning, cooking, and child care may seem intuitively obvious to women who have practiced these tasks since childhood. But for many guys like me, who never had a role model to insist I learn how to do these jobs, this work is not obvious at all. "We tend to avoid the things we can't do well," says Brohaugh. "Who likes to feel incompetent?"

We men, I suspect, are particularly phobic of this *incompetence* label. It's practically a cliché—for instance, how many of us would rather drive around in circles for hours before we stop to ask directions? Why? Because such would be a de facto admission we're lost. If you need further proof that the average guy will go to great lengths to avoid appearing a dufus, try this little experiment the next time you're at a party. Ask a man and a woman a question about a subject you know neither one knows anything about—for example, the Monte Carlo method for calculating equations of state. Odds are overwhelming that the woman will have no problem admitting her ignorance. Odds are equally overwhelming that the man will give you the benefit of his speculations—perhaps even, with a little encouragement, holding forth on the topic for the next half hour.

Besides stories from couples themselves, many of the upcoming chapters also include sections that fall into the category of *actionable advice* designed to help you not only change your minds about household work, but also change your behavior. Chapters 7 and 8 are primers on the basics of cleaning and cooking—primers designed to help the less domestically competent members of a household—often but not always the husband—get started on learning new skills. In some cases, these tips come from my own experience. In Chapter 7, for instance, you will see how I hired a professional maid—not to clean the house for me, but to teach me how to do it.

Other tips come directly from psychotherapists who have used a variety of proven approaches in their counseling—these are things that you can immediately begin trying in your own household. I can't emphasize this enough: Try different solutions. Some will work for you, others probably won't. But a flexible attitude on the part of all parties— one that's truly open to new possibilities—is a critical key to ending chore wars.

If there is one common element I found that successful households share, it's an agreement that the best tools for solving this problem are attitudes: kindness, flexibility, humor, and non-blaming pragmatism. You don't need to necessarily mimic anyone's solutions, but I highly recommend you work hard to mimic these can-do attitudes.

In short, *Chore Wars* is dedicated to helping people improve household harmony by:

- Coming to grips with the psychological aspects of chores inequity by discovering the ways men and women become locked into roles they often don't acknowledge exist;

- Encouraging less domestically involved spouses to move beyond helping at home to shouldering real responsibility for a share of the household workload (what one psychologist calls "owning" the tasks);

- Encouraging more domestically involved partners—usually but not always the woman—to acknowledge and begin to modify their own housework standards;

- Establishing a comprehensive inventory of your own household chores and responsibilities;

- Creating an efficient schedule for what jobs to do when throughout the year;

- Apportioning tasks in a way that minimizes a self-defeating score-keeping mentality;

- Providing men (and more than a few women) with a special how-to primer on domestic work—from laundry and dusting to simple cooking and child care—based on time-efficient advice from the pros;

- Lending inspiration through the stories of couples who have found greater happiness and satisfaction in their relationship after they learned how to reconfigure their approach to the domestic workload;

- Finally, showing people how they can actually feel good by sharing the management of a household they've created together.

DeVito Versus Redford: The Inside Story from the Marital Trenches

Change, of course, doesn't have to be a mirthless affair—if fact, you're more likely to succeed if all parties can maintain a sense of humor throughout the process. On this note, consider a poll conducted recently by Jim Sexton, currently an associate editor at *USA Today Weekend*, who designed the following when he was editor of *Special Report* magazine. Sexton wanted to get to "the murky heart of why men and women clash on chores." After surveying 555 randomly chosen married respondents, he found, among other things, that most men claim they do a fair share of domestic chores, while most women counter such claims by saying their partners do next to nothing at home. Sound familiar?

See if you recognize your own situation in the poll:

1. How much of the housework do you perform?

	WOMEN	MEN
Less than ¼	3%	14%
¼ to ½	6%	31%
½ to ¾	24%	40%
¾ or more	40%	7%
Everything	26%	6%

2. How much of the housework does your spouse perform?

	WOMEN	MEN
Less than ¼	49%	9%
¼ to ½	28%	13%
½ to ¾	19%	49%
¾ or more	2%	23%
Everything	0%	4%

3. How often should the toilet be cleaned?

WOMEN	MEN
96%	89%
said at least	said at least
once a week	once a week

4. When was the last time you cleaned the toilet?

WOMEN	MEN
89%	46%
had cleaned	had cleaned
the toilet in the	the toilet in the
last week (59%	last week (17%
said their husbands	said they had
had never cleaned	never cleaned
the toilet)	the toilet)

5. How often should the house be vacuumed?

WOMEN	MEN
95%	91%
said at least	said at least
once a week	once a week

6. When was the last time you vacuumed the house?

WOMEN	MEN
84%	60%
had vacuumed	had vacuumed
in the last week	in the last week
(27% said their	(7% said they
husbands had	had never
never vacuumed)	vacuumed)

7. How often should the car be washed?

WOMEN	MEN
85%	82%
said at least	said at least
once a month	once a month

8. When was the last time you washed the car?

WOMEN	MEN
61%	82%
had washed the car	had washed the car
in the last month	in the last month
(18% said they	(34% said their
had never	wives had never
washed the car)	washed the car)

9. How often should bed sheets be changed?

WOMEN	MEN
93%	90%
said at least	said at least
once a week	once a week

10. When was the last time you changed the sheets?

WOMEN
93%
had changed
the sheets in the
last week (53%
said their husbands
had never changed
the sheets)

MEN
57%
had changed
the sheets in the
last week (15%
said they had
never changed
the sheets)

11. How often should you clean out the refrigerator?

WOMEN
86%
said at least
once a month

MEN
82%
said at least
once a month

12. When was the last time you cleaned out the refrigerator?

WOMEN
88%
had cleaned out
the fridge in the
last month (68%
said their husbands
had never cleaned
out the fridge)

MEN
54%
had cleaned
out the fridge in
the last month
(24% said they
had never cleaned
out the fridge)

13. How long would it take to clean the house for a visit from your parents?

WOMEN
5.4 hours

MEN
3.5 hours

14. How long would it take to clean the house for a visit from your in-laws?

WOMEN
6.1 hours

MEN
3.7 hours

15. How long would it take to clean the house for a visit from out-of-town friends?

WOMEN	MEN
9.9 hours	6.5 hours

16. Would you rather take a sick child to the doctor's office or take the car in to be repaired?

WOMEN	MEN
74% Sick child	50% Sick child
22% Car repair	40% Car repair

17. Would you prefer an evening of lovemaking or a perfectly clean house?

	WOMEN	MEN
Lovemaking	46%	64%
Clean house	42%	26%
Don't know	12%	10%

18. Would you rather have okay sex in a clean house or great sex in a dirty house?

	WOMEN	MEN
Okay sex/clean house	53%	56%
Great sex/dirty house	31%	31%
Don't know	16%	14%

19. Would you rather your son learn to change the oil in the car or to do the ironing?

	WOMEN	MEN
Change the oil	57%	60%
Do the ironing	13%	13%
Both	27%	24%
Don't know	3%	3%

20. Would you rather your daughter learn to change the oil in the car or to do the ironing?

	WOMEN	MEN
Change the oil	18%	17%
Do the ironing	49%	56%
Both	30%	23%
Don't know	3%	4%

21. Do you ever argue with your spouse over household chores?

	WOMEN	MEN
Yes	42%	35%

22. How often are you angry with your spouse for not doing chores?

	WOMEN	MEN
All the time	10%	3%
Sometimes	21%	16%
Rarely	34%	32%
Never	32%	46%

23. Have you ever lost interest in sex because your spouse refused to do chores?

	WOMEN	MEN
Yes	7.2%	1.6%

24. How important is the cleanliness of your home to your self-esteem?

	WOMEN	MEN
Extremely important	32%	22%
Very important	53%	59%
Not very important	13%	14%
Not at all important	1%	4%

FOR WOMEN ONLY:

25. Would you rather marry a man who looks like Robert Redford but does no chores? Or a man who looks like Danny DeVito but does half the chores?

Robert Redford	46%
Danny DeVito	43%
Don't know	12%

26. In terms of chore habits, which character from *The Odd Couple* does your husband most resemble?

Felix Unger (the neat freak)	44%
Oscar Madison (the slob)	42%
Don't know	13%

27. Which do you find more appealing?

One who is washing dishes	61%
One who is dancing nude	24%

28. Would you rather have your house cleaned by your husband or your father?

Husband	81%
Father	11%
Don't know	8%

FOR MEN ONLY:

29. Have you ever worked late to avoid chores or performed a chore badly to get out of doing it again?

Worked late	14%
Botched chores	14%
Neither	75%
Don't know	2%

30. In terms of chore habits, which TV character does your wife most resemble?

June Cleaver	43%
Rosanne	24%
Don't know	33%

Hopefully, these amusing questions will get you and your spouse or housemates started on a constructive dialogue about how to make things fairer and better for you both. In the next chapter, we'll take a look at some of the surprising psychological and physical benefits of housework—and help you better gauge how much of a problem chore wars is in your household.

Chapter 2

ASSESSING THE BATTLEFIELD

Where Does *Your* Household Fall?

A desire to resist oppression is implanted in the nature of man.
—Tacitus

Attention to detail and deriving pleasure from the task itself are things I have learned from my husband. It sounds a little sappy, but it's true that we integrate most household 'chores' into our living to an unusual extent. This is really a wonderful aspect of our domestic relationship, because an enormous amount of tension is eliminated.
—Cathryn S.

If anything, I have tried to encourage my husband to relax his standards. He is definitely much more particular than I, but has learned to be less demanding.
—Heather F.

I do it all, and not very well.
—Rhedd L.

A good starting point for setting a truce in the chore wars seems at first glance laughably obvious: determining if a problem even exists for you. For couples like Tony and Lorraine, who in the past have written about their different points of view for *Glamour,* the problem is as impossible to ignore as a magnified dust mite:

Tony's Story

"Why does it take two people at least four hours a week to clean a small-ish house that doesn't even contain children? Because we clean it to her standards. Lorraine's. My wife's.

"Yes. I am that rare and precious thing, a man ready to do house-work. But willingly? No. I do it because we both work at home and create roughly equal messes, so it seems only fair that we both get involved in cleaning them up. Besides, if I didn't, I would get nothing but brussels sprouts for dinner when it's her turn to cook.

"But why do we have to clean once a week? Why not every ten days, or even every two weeks? Do we have to dust all the surfaces each time?

"I don't have answers to any of these questions. I am hardly even allowed to ask them. Take the back of the stove. The back of the stove has a little ledge, and she keeps a carton of salt there, a pot of honey, a sugar bowl and creamer from her childhood home (one shaped like a chicken, the other like a rooster), and a box of Jane's Krazy Mixed-Up Salt (salt with herbs). When you lift those things up, behold: There are marks underneath that fit the outlines of their bottoms. It is my job to clean these marks up every week . . . *But if you don't lift them up, the ledge on the back of the stove looks perfectly clean.* So I ask you (I can't ask her)—why lift them up?

"Cleaning the stove is one of my jobs. She likes to walk around and say, 'Your job is to hang up the clothes.' Or, 'Your job is to dust the leaves on the philodendron.' Okay, we don't have a philodendron, but you get the idea: She's the boss. By executive decision—hers. But both of us signed the mortgage on this place. We both cry when the roof starts to leak. So where is it written that the house should be cleaned to her specs?

"Lorraine is a stickler about dust. To her it's the enemy. She worries about dust mites, which are so tiny they can live on dust, but which, when you magnify them a million times, look like giant crabs with enormous claws that are gonna get you. I say, don't magnify them. And when we dust, we have to use a dust rag. The gold kind impregnated with some sort of oil.

"If I had my way, cleaning the house would not be such an intense and exhausting experience. But I don't get my way. I have no standing when it comes to dirt. Who made her the boss of clean?"

Lorraine's Story

"When I met this man he was conducting mold experiments—green fuzz was multiplying in little plastic boxes in the back of the refrigerator. 'What is it?' I asked, holding one up. 'Uhhh . . . what do you think?' he asked sheepishly. He can feign sheepish better than the dog, and that is saying something. It could have been broccoli; it could have been spaghetti sauce; it could have been a bugging device planted by his last girlfriend.

"She had moved out six months earlier, and, 'Alas!' he said, '*She took the vacuum cleaner.*'

"And the dog ate your homework, you poor boy! Assorted bits of sand, dirt, dried food bits, juices, what have you, congealed into a hard paste, some paper scraps, and a couple dozen dust balls cohabiting on the kitchen floor! (Did this woman also take the broom?) Newspapers stacked chest high on the landing in case he forgot to clip something important. (You can't be too hasty, he explained.) Dust so thick on tables you could almost see the mites plying their trade. The bathroom I won't discuss.

"Just what was the guy's filth-tolerance level? We must be from different planets. Certainly he was violating the health code. That's probably why he first brought me there in the dead of the night. If this relationship was going to survive more than forty-eight hours, he was going to have to edge—no gallop—closer to my housekeeping standards. This was a non-negotiable demand. (What I hadn't told him yet was that I am allergic to dust.)

"At first he joined me in cleaning without complaint. This guy has potential, I said to myself. This can work. We got things straightened out in a few days—he was quite surprised at how happy neighbors are to lend vacuum cleaners—and he seemed quite pleased with the change in his apartment.

"But then what did he do? He filled my head with pretty lies! He complimented my domestic skills. He told me that I made the place ever so much more livable than the previous female inhabitant—a most welcome comparison, which I foolishly took to heart. I didn't for a minute think he was tricking me when he asked: 'How does the washing machine work? How much soap should I use? Should I wash the pants I wore when I changed the oil in the car in the same load as your Victoria's Secret underwear?' I was too smart for that kind of thing.

"In short, he bamboozled me into thinking that he welcomed my taking charge, and since he had acted like the good soldier, working alongside me, I assumed that my donning the mantle of housekeeping maven—that my making all *executive decisions* regarding cleaning— would satisfy our domestic needs.

"Of course, what I didn't count on is that being executive housekeeper with a greater penchant for neatness than my underling also meant that I, alas, would wind up doing more of the work."

Hot War, Cold War: How Big Is Your Problem?

For many men who read Tony's and Lorraine's diametrical views of housework, a certain sympathy for Tony's plight is inescapable. *Right on!* some of you are probably thinking. *Call in the National Guard and set this guy free from his slave master!*

Many women, on the other hand, are likely to feel Lorraine's pain as acutely as their own. *How can that slob be so blind to dirt? He's probably clueless, as well, about how exhausting it is not only to do the vast majority of the work, but also to be responsible for all of it!*

Such blood-boiling stories are by no means rare in the popular media, which seem to thrive on gender warfare, the more incendiary, the better. Dirt-blind husbands and bone-tired wives have become a virtual staple of women's magazines, right up there with stories on cellulite creams and ways to improve your sex life. But the commonness of such stories doesn't always reflect the reality experienced by many men and women in relationships.

The truth is there are many couples, traditional or otherwise, for whom the division of housework is simply not an unending nightmare. This is because both partners have agreed upon, consciously or not, a division of household work that both can live with. Neither feels particular resentment about this division, and neither feels particular guilt. And so the household runs more or less smoothly most of the time.

Synchronous Standards

Perhaps the single greatest predictor of a household's degree of domestic tranquility is whether or not the adult inhabitants share a vision of what constitutes a properly kept home. (Kids, of course, be they tots or teens, are likely to have their own ideal home concepts, too, but as long as their parents present a reasonably united front, youngsters can learn to respect this.)

As The Odd Couple so amusingly illustrated, people's "mess tolerance" can range widely, from those who feel comfortable only if their kitchen floor is spotless enough to eat off of, to those who feel comfortable eating off the kitchen floor because that's where the food is most likely to be found. "We're very lucky," says Andrew about his relationship with Trish. "We're both neat people, and we agree on how our house should look."

"If Andy *didn't* share my view," says Trish, "I think we would really have a lot more problems."

Not that mess-divergent folks can't eventually find common ground. "We definitely started out with vastly different tolerance levels for cleanliness and clutter, but that has moderated over the years of our marriage," says Marcia, an insurance company executive. "To give you an example, when Joe and I first met, he was living in a small studio apartment on East 10th Street in New York City. He basically had a bed, a

Formica table, and chairs. The prospect of my first visit over there, he told me years later, caused him to launder his sheets for the first time in months. In his fridge, he had only orange juice and beer, and his tub needed that special high-grade cleanser 'Zud.' Over the years, and particularly with the advent of children, I have learned to tolerate our place's being less neat and clean than I would like. And Joe, for his part, has learned a higher level of neatness."

Adds Joe, a banker: "When Marty and I first moved in together, I expected few surprises. We had stayed at each other's places scores of times during the previous year, and I thought we had seen each other under virtually all possible conditions. But while moving Marty's stuff to our three-room flat above an old mattress factory on the Lower East Side, I grabbed a small denim bag, with a shoulder strap, that must have weighed fifteen pounds. It was stuffed with tools—hammers, screw drivers, pliers, tape, screws, nails, you name it. I was amazed. At the time, I had three tools in my possession: a calculator, a typewriter, and a roach clip. They had gotten me everything I had ever needed since I left my mother's home.

"As a young adult, home for me wasn't where you hung your hat—it was where you ended up when you had absolutely nothing else to do. I once moved out of an apartment because the rent was going from $90 to $100 a month. The whole idea of paying three figures a month, just for a place to crash, was ridiculous. One-room flats, attic apartments, barracks, dormitories—these were the only kind of places I had lived in for the last decade. To ultimately live in a four-bedroom house with a spouse and children was a change of such magnitude that it was hard to fathom. I knew I wasn't going to become some kind of anal-retentive house boy, but I realized I would never live that way again."

Just as couples (not to mention dog owners) are said to start physically resembling one another after years of being together, so do their household standards usually undergo a natural kind of moderation toward the mean. In our own marriage, Debbie and I consider ourselves lucky because we now both fit somewhere in the middle of the neatness and cleanliness spectrum. We're not slobs, exactly, despite what our relatives might say. But neither are we at high risk of developing obsessive-compulsive cleaning rituals in the near future.

For us, reaching a comfortable, agreed upon equilibrium point seemed to occur without much conscious effort. This is probably because our standards were reasonably close to begin with. Now, when the clutter becomes too much for me, I launch into a straightening blitzkrieg—and when the dust bunnies reach the size of the kids' stuffed animals, Debbie goes wild with the vacuum cleaner. On such occasions, we're naturally both grateful for each other's efforts, but most of the time, we're content to live in a home we both find clean and neat *enough*.

Would we prefer to have our house kept as impeccably as Windsor Castle? Probably. Can we live with something that falls far short of this ideal, especially if it means we both have more time to pursue other interests? Definitely.

For couples who really do resemble the extremes of Oscar and Felix, however, finding common ground can involve hard work and real compromise. Still, as you will see in coming chapters, it *can* be done—even where divorce itself seems the only cure.

Complementary Labor

Having standards that are in the same ballpark is not the only key to relationships relatively untroubled by chore wars. To be sure, there are many situations where both parties are neat freaks—and yet one person (usually the man) will hardly lift a finger to help bring this about. Only when a mutual attitude is reinforced by action is domestic tranquility likely to flourish. Having said this, it's important to point out that the action need not be identical.

Explains Eric, a forty-eight-year-old veterinarian from the Boston area who is married to an intensive care nurse, "Sylvia and I both work outside the home, and we both work inside the home. Practically from the time we met, we vowed to share equally the responsibilities for rearing our children, earning a living, and doing the dreaded chores. This doesn't mean we split everything down the middle. Over time, we've learned what each of us does best. I am a macro cleaner, for instance, and Sylvia follows me up as a detail person."

Adds Sylvia: "We've been married for twenty-five years now, and we're both very comfortable with our division of work. Maybe we're just lucky, but there really are no chore wars here."

As Eric and Sylvia's experience suggests, sharing the chores does not mean each does precisely 50 percent of every given task. Nor is their division based on a more complicated mathematical equality—that is, he does A chores for B duration with median degree of difficulty C for an overall burden/satisfaction score of D; and she does W chores for X duration with median degree of difficulty Y for an overall burden/satisfaction score of Z.

Before you get out a calculator or purchase a software program to try to reconcile D and Z, realize that math is not the arbiter here—emotions are. Time and again, the couples and therapists I interviewed stressed this point: What *feels* fair and right to both has virtually nothing to do with by-the-numbers equality. And what feels right is the point.

Silver Linings

Many couples at peace with each other and their roles at home also share an unconventional view of chores. Rather than viewing these as nothing but burdensome drudgery, they actually see a variety of *benefits* in undertaking the many jobs of the household, benefits that range from the psychological and the physical to the romantic.

Hard as it may be for the more slovenly among us to understand, some men and women actually find it psychologically soothing to clean and straighten up a disheveled home. Fans of the old *Mary Tyler Moore Show* will no doubt remember how Mary Richards flew into a frenzy of house cleaning whenever her stress level got the best of her.

Arguably, there are a lot of Marys among us. "I definitely find it relaxing to clean my house when there's excessive stress in my life," says Liza Taylor, a horticulturist from Pittsburgh. "The fact that it's mindless work is not a drawback for me—it's a plus. The truth is I find it very satisfying to just putter around the house, bringing order to disorder. I put my stereo on, and, as I lose myself in the tasks and the music, it takes my mind off my worries."

Explains psychotherapist Gail Hartman, "You can't discount the fact that for a lot of individuals, housework is not so much drudgery as a way of exerting control over their environment. Housework can actually reduce anxiety." It's a psychological boost that men as well as women are likely to seek out. Explains Wallace, a self-described neatnik living with Priscilla, a self-described slob, "The truth is, I enjoy housework—lucky for her. I like to impose order on chaos, so to speak. Once you get your routines down, so you no longer have to think about what you're doing, it even has a Zen aspect to it. It's very meditative.

"I highly recommend it, especially for the type-A guy who doesn't know how to relax. I would say to such a guy: Learn to bake yourself some bread. Iron your own shirts, you big baby. What the hell, be a real man and change your own oil. After all, life is about 20 percent growth and 80 percent maintenance. You might as well get used to it."

Shaping Up the House— While Shaping Up Yourself

Housework can also be an unexpectedly good way to stay physically fit. The American College of Sports Medicine and the Centers for Disease Control and Prevention recently issued a joint policy recommendation urging all Americans to get regular, moderate exercise for at least thirty minutes each day. The recommendation added that this exercise doesn't have to be done all at once—it can be spread out over the course of the day.

Traditional exercises, from jogging to swimming, are fine, of course—but so are less obvious workouts like gardening and housework. One researcher found that men and women who expend 2,000 calories a week in such pursuits can significantly reduce the risk of heart disease, stroke, diabetes, colon cancer, and clinical depression—and add two years to their lives.

Another researcher, Dr. Arthur Leon at University of Minnesota, found that very moderate exercise, such as gardening and working around your yard or house for forty-five minutes a day, reduces overall death rates by 20 percent and heart disease deaths by 30 percent.

Arguably, women *are* getting more of these benefits than their couch potato male counterparts. Dr. William L. Haskell, a Stanford University

Medical School professor, recently equipped 111 men and ninety-four women to devices that record motion and heart rate throughout the day. The results: Overall, women used 20 percent more of their aerobic capacity than men, a difference the researchers felt was due in large part to the greater quantity of household chores performed by women.

Sure, both men and women can increase their aerobic capacity by plodding to nowhere on the treadmill at the local gym. Or you can do the kind of exercise that shapes up more than just your physique.

From Dust to Trust—
The Emotional and Romantic Benefits

For many people, successfully reconfiguring their approach to housework can have a profoundly uplifting effect on their relationship. Just as many working women have gained self-esteem from their successes on the job, so too have many men derived measurable mental health benefits from assuming a greater share of domestic and parenting duties.

In her research on working couples, Nancy Marshall, Ed.D., of the Wellesley College Center for Research on Women, found that the more activities a person is involved in—career, intimate relationship, parenting, and the like—the stronger his or her sense of identity and well-being tends to be. To be sure, Marshall concedes, the busier your life gets, the greater the chance that you will have some hellishly stressful days. On the other hand, the more you do, the more likely that *something* in your life will be going right. "Our research," says Marshall, "shows over and over again that the benefits of multiple roles for males and females alike outweigh the stresses."

So, for every guy who has tucked away in the back of his brain, I pose this question: *You want me to change—but what's in it for me?* The answer is *plenty*. Take Aaron, for instance, a forty-three-year-old father of three who grew up in Boston during the heyday of *Leave It to Beaver*. By today's standards, Aaron says, his own boyhood upbringing was "sexist beyond words—100 percent of the cooking, cleaning, making beds, and so on was handled by my mother. Dad was responsible for woodworking, lawn mowing, painting—the testosterone stuff, the work that can only be done if you have thick tufts of hair on your back. Dad had a full-time job as a stockbroker; Mom was a full-time Mom—it was kind of like a 1950s TV family."

In the years since Aaron and his working wife, Jill, have been together, Aaron admits to radically altering his standards on the home-front—first just to bring them into compliance with the state's public health code, but eventually to bring them closer to his wife's wishes. "During college, when my wife and I were still dating, I'd have mounds of bug-infested dust, old newspapers, damp towels, diseased orange rinds and pizza crusts, and fetid socks adorning my dorm room floor. I swear, it must have been the breeding ground for the Ebola virus; you'd want to venture into my dorm room in a Hot Zone suit. But I've been won over to my wife's view of cleanliness. I now believe, for instance, that a stray pair of underwear *belongs* in a laundry bag, rather than my former belief that underthings could rest perfectly comfort-ably on a bookshelf or atop a VCR or alongside the lettuce in the salad crisper."

Aaron jokes that his metamorphosis occurred via a process much like training a seal. But the real reason, he admits, was that it dawned on him that this was one of the best ways he could make his wife happy—and her happiness, in turn, rebounded back to him. "To this day," he says, "my wife insists that men are never more handsome than when they are washing the evening dishes. So I wash the dishes *a lot.*"

I, too, found my own evolution from career-minded drudge (with few other interests beyond financial ambition) to a significantly more active participant in the life of our household at once humbling, eye-opening, and ultimately inspiring. I don't mean to sound like a SNAG here (Sensitive New Age Guy), but I do love my wife, and I believe the more you give in your relationship, the more you tend to get in return.

Don't Deny Your Denial

Unfortunately, despite all the benefits that can accrue to both partners when the load is shared, the distribution of work continues to be quite unequal in the overwhelming majority of cases. If you're a man, you're quite possibly now thinking, "Yeah, I can see that. Most guys probably do delude themselves into thinking they *do* more work at home than they *actually* do. But fortunately for us, that's not me. In our household, my wife and I share things equally. She probably does a little more than me—something on the order of 52 percent her, 48 percent me."

At the end of this chapter, you'll have the chance to test out these percentages a little more rigorously. But first consider the revealing stories of Jacob and Jane, a couple whose domestic arrangement is very close to parity (he says) and very far from it (she says).

Jacob's Story

"While our relationship has been visited by probably not an atypical range of debates, tensions, and trials, the fact is that the constellations have so arranged themselves in the remarkable way that we have practically no problems surrounding chores. I attribute this to two factors.

"First, I work like a dog (a very aesthetically sensitive dog) so that we have enough money to pay for housecleaning once every two weeks and for intermittent chores such as window washing and minor household repairs.

"Secondly, and more remarkably, we have complementary thresholds for sensing when a chore might be needed. Jane always rushes to cook or do laundry or go marketing long before I sense there is any need for this. I, on the other hand, am an expert at sweeping crumbs off floors, vacuuming rugs after children have left bits of paper, stickers, and crumbs on them, and cleaning closets and cupboards. Thus we are both happy at all times because we like doing all of the chores that we think are necessary.

"A typical event in our household may find Jane working at the kitchen counter. She has four pots and skillets on the stove cooking for a typical weekday meal, and she is now preparing a salad. She does not notice that she is standing on a floor covered with bits of food, bread crumbs, scraps of paper, little black bits of unknown origin, crushed crayons, and dried yogurt. She would not notice this accumulation unless it approached her ankles or one of her relatives was about to visit.

"I notice this, of course, immediately, and use whatever combination of whisking and scrubbing is necessary to clean it, all the while expecting a peanut butter sandwich for dinner. In a few minutes—voila! A great dinner and a clean floor, a happy couple, and no chore debates!"

Jane's Story

"The main difference between our responsibilities is the nature of the duties we perform: mine are generally daily, while Jacob's are intermittent and somewhat optional. I don't remember ever discussing whose responsibility many of the chores are. Mostly, it comes down to who's more concerned about a particular chore, and who's more available to do it. The bottom line is that I end up shouldering much more of the burden.

"For instance, one of my main chores is picking up—clearing shoes, toys, clothes, and stray pieces of things (embroidery thread, beads, puzzle pieces, parts of torn book pages, single socks, dress-up accessories . . .) from stairs, floors, tables, and beds. If I don't do these things daily, our house seems distressingly messy to me and our life just too disordered. Picking up doesn't take long, but it's a constant, annoying obligation. I do it because clutter doesn't seem to bother Jacob. This not-minding-messiness is a handy masculine trait.

"A larger, but more interesting, daily chore is kitchen work. I love to cook, plan meals, and shop for food, so I have always taken care of all these things. Once in a blue moon—like our first overnight date, Jacob proves himself surprisingly competent at cooking. Nowadays, though, he's more likely to just bring home Chinese.

"Since our three small children vastly prefer Kraft macaroni and cheese to spinach and black bean burritos, my time in the kitchen has increased in volume and decreased in interest. There's more food to buy, carry, unpack, and prepare, and a lot less pleasure in doing so.

"The good news is that Jacob now does the dinner dishes, or at least some of them, on a pretty regular basis. Since I may have done one or two loads of dishes already (by trying to cook things the kids do like,

like homemade applesauce, bread, or any dessert), it's a help. I do, however, resent the lack of acknowledgment on Jacob's part of the kitchen work I do.

"My other main chore is the laundry. I take it to the basement, sort it, wash about ten loads a week, fold it up, and return the clothes to their proper drawers. I actually like to do laundry—it's sort of relaxing. But, of course, it cuts into the amount of time I could spend doing other things, such as, say, haiku-writing.

"Jacob handles dry cleaning and the servicing of the car. He'll also go to the grocery store if I give him a small list. His other responsibilities tend to fall into the home maintenance category: changing the furnace filter; installing the heat cable on our roof; dealing with weatherstripping and window screens; fiddling with the furnace; and fixing broken doorknobs. Even though each of these items may take up no more than a half hour annually, I am extraordinarily grateful to him for doing them.

"We used to alternate the bill-paying, but Jacob does it all now on the computer. I didn't mind it—and secretly thought I did it more efficiently. I do, however, continue to manage our stocks. I enjoy following them and making the occasional trade.

"As for child care, I do the vast majority of it. But Jacob is an excellent father with a great rapport with the kids, and he is very willing to spend time with them when he's not at the office. One year, we gave each other semiannual 'weekends alone,' during which one of us would go somewhere alone and the other would keep the kids. Though this was my idea, which actually came out of desperation and exhaustion, Jacob went along with it, and we each enjoyed a couple of weekends of sleeping late and going to the movies (albeit without each other).

"The best way I've found to modify Jacob's behavior has been to talk openly and calmly about any problems as we see them. If this fails, nagging has also proved fairly helpful, believe it or not—although one must be persistent for years and have a loving spouse who would rather change than be nagged. You can also try a little peer pressure, which can work wonders. All the other men we know do the dishes for their wives, and some of them cook, too."

Take the Test

As the perspectives of Jacob and Jane suggest, often only one of the combatants in chore wars—that is, the consistently overburdened—truly considers domestic workload inequality to be a war. The ones whose torsos are most likely to have left a divot on the TV room couch may have a vague sense that something's not working. But odds are whatever this *something* is, it's best handled by not focusing too much attention on it.

This ostrich-like strategy of denial is something I am intimately familiar with—for years, I truly believed that I did close to half of our family's household chores. Now I know I wasn't even coming close—a fact that was *always* obvious to Debbie.

As a partial antidote to what is most often manly denial, I strongly urge you and your housemates take the following quiz that ranks twenty-eight common household tasks, each assigned a different difficulty point value. To get these rankings, 555 respondents—296 women and 259 men—rated each of the tasks on a scale of one to ten, with one being a cakewalk, and ten being a giant pain in the neck. Jim Sexton, who designed the quiz, then averaged the responses to come up with an unbiased figure.

To take the quiz, check the chores that you do and the ones your mate performs (if you share a chore, you can split the point value); then total your points. "Now it is possible," says Sexton with a chuckle, "to finally prove—scientifically and beyond a shadow of a doubt—that you do more housework than your partner does."

CHORES	YOU	MATE	POINT VALUE
1. Taking the kids to soccer practice			2
2. Changing the sheets			3
3. Gardening, inside and out			3
4. Making minor household repairs			3

CHORES	YOU	MATE	POINT VALUE
5. Recycling			3
6. Taking the kids to the doctor			3
7. Vacuuming			3
8. Buying birthday presents			4
9. Changing diapers			4
10. Cooking dinner			4
11. Doing the laundry			4
12. Dusting			4
13. Shopping for groceries			4
14. Taking out the garbage			4
15. Washing the car			4
16. Cleaning the sinks and tubs			5
17. Mopping			5
18. Mowing the yard			5
19. Washing dishes			5
20. Washing the pet			5
21. Dealing with repairmen			6
22. Paying the bills			6

CHORES	YOU	MATE	POINT VALUE
23. Changing the oil			7
24. Cleaning out the refrigerator			7
25. Ironing			7
26. Cleaning the toilet			8
27. Cleaning the oven			10
28. Washing windows, inside and out			10

TOTALS: **YOU** _____   **MATE** _____

Now that you've totaled your scores, you may be noting a somewhat more substantial gap than both of you originally predicted. In the next chapter, we'll look at some of the surprisingly powerful psychological issues that surround housework—and strategies you can use to begin defusing them.

Chapter 3

WHEN YOU'RE READY FOR A TRUCE
Seeing the Big Picture

Where there are two, one cannot be wretched and one not.
—Euripides

*For a male and female to live continuously together is . . .
biologically speaking, an extremely unnatural condition.*
—Robert Briffault

*Nothing is really work unless you would rather be doing
something else.*
—James Barrie

*Be satisfied with success in even the smallest matter,
and think that even such a result is no trifle.*
—Marcus Aurelius

*My standards have never been as high as my wife's. I have
accepted her standards as our ultimate objective. But I believe
she has made some progress in accepting that in striving for
perfection, it is okay to live with a near miss.*
—Lee T.

Natalie's Story

"The domestic work is divided pretty unequally at our house. I do most of it. Don loves to cook and he certainly loves our daughter, but cleaning—not so much. It mostly boils down to time. Don's been working long hours to start a new business, so I have more of it. I also actually enjoy doing all those domestic things, and I care at lot more than Don whether or not they're done.

"The truth is I am becoming increasingly comfortable with the idea that I am domestic. And that doesn't mean I'm not professional or intelligent or liberated. I do more because I'm home more, I like it, I'm good at it, and I have a head for details.

"But having said this, I don't like being in charge of everything. In fact, the incredibly lopsided division of work is really the main stress that wracks our relationship. I know Don has feelings of guilt, and my feelings are definitely of resentment.

"Several times a year, I usually initiate an 'OK, this is it' conversation where we proceed to come up with a new plan (usually a new list of chores for Don to complete with a timetable for him to do them). Obviously, it hasn't completely worked.

"I should point out that it is not the physical work itself that I end up feeling stiffed over. In fact, it's actually cathartic for me. When we had a house cleaner for six months, I actually missed the housework! What really gets me is having to be responsible for all the details: for example, remembering to put out the recycling, picking up milk, sending mom (his mom) a birthday card, changing the toilet paper roll when it's empty, and so on.

"I have been told, 'If he loves you, and he knows it's important to you, he will help even if it isn't so important to him.' The big question is whether it's too much to expect Don to notice, much less do anything about, these various tasks.

"When I reach the point where I feel like I just can't absorb another detail, we talk. It's not that Don can't take responsibility for some of this. When the baby and I went away for a week last summer, we came home to a completely well-managed home. What a wonderful feeling it was! And Don ended up being thankful to me as well. He told me he finally realized how much work running the house takes, a concept that had apparently never graced his thoughts before.

"Unfortunately, when I'm around, Don seems to lose much of his incentive for taking charge of household matters. He will do anything I tell him to, but I absolutely try to steer clear of nagging and giving directions. I haven't *purposely* tried to modify Don's behavior, although, when I do reach my breaking point, he becomes extremely helpful in order to diffuse my anger and, at least for a while, to make amends. (I *wouldn't* suggest this as a course of action, however.)

"After my last blow-up, Don posted a list on the fridge, *his* ideas of what *maybe* should be done around the house, things he feels that *maybe* he should be responsible for. They include drilling, pounding, measuring, and dismantling. He also tries to cook something yummy on the weekends.

"We were both brought up in homes where our moms handled the cooking, cleaning, and kids, and our dads did the cars, yard, and plumbing. And while we are definitely influenced by that, I don't think either of us believes that is the way it should be or even the way we want it to be. In theory, I have always wanted to have an equal share sort of marriage. In reality, I am doing more.

"I find myself wishing that Don would just be a little more aware of all the daily tasks I handle—with some more frequent 'thank you's' thrown in. I *am* very careful to thank Don (and I really am thankful for what he does) on a regular basis in front of our daughter, to reinforce to them both that I appreciate what he does. 'Thanks' goes a long way for me. I wish he would reciprocate."

Don's Story

"Household chores? Couldn't we talk about something a little more pleasant, like war and famine? Honestly, this has been a sore subject lately.

"Not that we fight about chores. In fact, there's really little to argue about. Natalie does practically everything. By comparison, I do practically nothing. The difference is I know it. I feel like a slug, and the guilt drives me crazy.

"I think Nat is much more preoccupied with the everyday needs of the family. She anticipates grocery and shopping needs and has higher standards of cleanliness and organization. Consequently, she senses what needs to be done long before I do. And if she asks me to help, I gladly will. What she resents is that she has to think of everything. She's told me on several occasions that if I were to take the initiative more often, that would go a long way toward making her feel better.

"We seem to have fallen into a routine that goes something like this: Nat does most of the work, including laundry, cleaning, and taking care of the baby, while I take out the occasional bag of garbage or recyclables. On the surface, all is well for a few months, until she reaches critical mass and in a fit of tears tells me that, for all the help I'm providing, she might as well be a single parent. After that, I'm a model husband for several days. But eventually, we slip back into the same routine.

"Things are complicated by biweekly visits from the in-laws. During their visits, they take care of many special projects, like installing new locks or repairing the porch windows or simply helping out by watching our baby girl. This is helpful, to be sure, but it also shows me up. I am not nearly as helpful a husband as my father-in-law is.

"As long as I'm making excuses: I have been spending most of my time trying to start up a new business. That has left most of the day-to-day work to Natalie. However, now that the business is showing signs of stability, I have been able to come home at a relatively decent hour—6:00 P.M.—and help out.

"It doesn't help either that I come from a family where the work is split between my mother and, well, my mother. She does virtually everything. My father has his odd projects, like working on the cars or building terraces in the backyard. But, since he is terribly inefficient in how he does these projects (Case in point: The house he built in 1976 is still unfinished!), his 'contributions' only add to the stress load. Even as I was growing up, my load of chores was light. My mother—the perfect Peruvian mother—took good care of her boy.

"I am like my father in that I don't have much fondness for housework. We would both rather read newspapers, magazines, or books, or watch a documentary. We are both information sponges and put a much higher priority on learning. Lately, though, I've come to think that having such priorities is a luxury afforded only when someone else does the work.

"I do feel that I am on the road to turning over a new leaf, so to speak. The change is not so much external, but in my own head. I have begun to think of familial duties as something that I need to be concerned with—if only to be a good husband and father.

"After our last blowout, I suggested that perhaps my problem could be remedied with a *list*. My reasoning was that, even if things that need doing come to mind, I don't always remember long enough to take action. As an old Chinese proverb goes: The weakest ink is stronger than the best memory.

"With a list of chores, perhaps I will be able to see what needs doing. I'm looking at the list right now. It has only two items to date, both of them crossed off: 'Superglue the toy bin to the shower wall' and 'Drain the hot water heater.'

"Honestly, I enjoyed the feeling of domesticity when I put those items on the list. And it's been encouraging to see the items crossed off—evidence of having done something tangible. Unfortunately, I seem to have exhausted all the available chores in the house. Guess I'll read the paper until something comes up."

Searching for Answers in an Age of Overload

Couples like Don and Natalie are legion today—people who obviously love and respect each other, but for whom the issue of household labor hangs like a mildly toxic fog over their home. Both of them are, on some level, truly committed to making things better; in fact, they've tried—probably on a dozen or more occasions—to come up with strategies to fix this problem.

And though solutions like Don's list may seem promising at first, a true resolution is elusive—a will-o'-the-wisp that tends to evaporate quickly beneath the grinding momentum of daily life. A cycle sets in: Resentment leads to a blowup, which leads to an "answer," which is gradually forgotten, which leads to more resentment. With each turn of the cycle, both people feel more hopeless and more convinced that there is no way out.

Exacerbating this cycle further is the often crushing level of stress American families experience today. If you and your mate both have careers, you already know how overwhelming some days can be. Stress at work percolating over to home and vice versa, and your kids with their own host of needs and demands: There's a definite decapitated-chicken quality to modern life that leaves many of us bouncing off the walls in a reactive frenzy, no brain left to make sense of our predicament.

Against this backdrop of befuddling pressures, it's easy to focus on the minutiae of dirty dishes and unfolded socks and miss the larger picture. But the chore wars don't exist in a vacuum—they are part of a larger societal phenomenon, that is, the shift away from once clearly defined gender roles and expectations.

Says sociologist Arlie Hochschild: "Every American household bears the footprints of economic and cultural trends that originate far outside its walls." Inflation and global economic competition, for instance, have significantly eroded male wages, forcing many men to work harder just to keep from falling behind. In recent decades, women in steadily escalating numbers have joined the workforce, spurred in part by the opportunities opened up to them by the women's movement, and in part because two paychecks are necessary for many families to stay afloat.

But even as more and more women are joining men, by choice or necessity, as breadwinners, past gender roles and attitudes are not so easily shed. For both spouses, chore wars are multifaceted and pernicious—a problem with many aspects, which themselves tend to interact and compound the sense of being overwhelmed. A dirty kitchen floor and a boss' harsh word may seem, at first, completely unrelated—but chances are your nervous system won't agree.

Complicating matters even more is the fact that men and women do not always react the same to work and home stresses—much as we might hope, in today's increasingly egalitarian world, that we *should*. Focusing only on chore wars—without taking into consideration the larger context within which these flourish—gives at best a myopic view of the problem.

The French have an expression: *Tout comprendre, c'est tout pardonner* (if you understand everything, you forgive everything). This expression doesn't *entirely* apply to men and women in the throes of chore wars. In such cases, to be sure, understanding only goes so far. Still, when spouses understand and empathize with what the other is going through emotionally both at home and at work, it helps eliminate needless and self-defeating misinterpretations of behavior. (*He won't help because he doesn't care about me*, or, *The last thing I need is another bad boss at home—why can't she give me a half hour to unwind before starting in on me?*)

Similarly, by understanding how your spouse best copes with stress, you can better help her regain her bearings—and in so doing, set the scene for greater household productivity. It may seem a peripheral way to approach washing the toilet, but let's face it: When someone is a stressed-out wreck, chances are that housework won't be a high priority. It's as true in a household as it is in a company—workers under too much stress are poor performers. Therefore, the more you can help assuage your partner's overall stress level, the more she will be ready, willing, and able to contribute productively at home.

To better understand the big picture of stress in two-career couples, consider how home and work problems intertwine to impact the lives of several couples:

Scenes from a Marriage

After seventeen years of marriage, Betsy Mulligan can tell at a glance when her husband, Tom, has had an overwhelming day at the supercomputer company where he works as a middle manager. "You can just see it," says the thirty-nine-year-old social worker. "He sits on the couch surrounded by unfinished work. His head hangs down, and he just looks sad."

On such nights—which have been increasingly frequent during recent slumping sales of supercomputers—Betsy says she tries to give her stressed husband a break from his share of the household duties. She cooks dinner, washes the dishes, and puts their three children to bed by herself, allowing Tom time to mentally unwind.

But when it's Betsy who's stressed out from work problems of her own, Tom, thirty-eight, admits he does not always precisely reciprocate her efforts on the homefront. Several weeks ago, for instance, Betsy had a horrible day at the walk-in therapy center where she works part-time as a counselor for severely disturbed patients. In the course of one session, a male patient became verbally abusive, accusing her of incompetence and threatening her. Compounding this tension was an upcoming exam Betsy was studying for day and night in order to become a licensed psychotherapist.

When Tom came home that evening, he could immediately sense from her body language that something was wrong. "When I walked in, the kids were all in the kitchen, and I could see that Betsy was stressed out," he recalls. "She'd taken a practice exam, and it didn't go well. I said, 'Can I help out here?' But it just did not click. She gave me a couple things to do to pitch in, but it's just not a natural thing for me to come in and take over at home."

Tom says he *did* volunteer to make dinner that night.

Recalls Betsy with a weary smile, "Actually, you said, 'Let's go out for dinner.' I ended up making dinner myself, but we went out for dessert."

Unequal as this may seem on the face of it, both spouses agree that Tom works far longer hours outside of the home than Betsy now does, though she expects this will change as she gets back into the workforce full-time. "When I was home all the time with our kids," she says, "it made more sense for me to be running everything here. But as I am making this change and going back to work now, it's difficult to make the shifts at home because the patterns are so set."

Still, Betsy admits that not all the difficulties in adjusting workloads are Tom's. As much as she wants domestic equality, she does not always make it easy for her husband to help out. "I tend to be fairly controlling at home," Betsy says. "I want things run my way, and in a sense I don't want to give up that authority."

"It's just not that black and white an issue," adds Tom, and Betsy nods in agreement.

At this, the couple's oldest daughter, Sarah, twelve, enters the kitchen to say good night. "We'll tuck you in," says Tom, who pauses a beat before adding, "one of these days."

"Ha, ha," says Sarah as she heads off for bed by herself.

Golden Rule

Bridget and Ross Hollander have a rule in their marriage: Whoever suffers the more stressful day at work gets pampered by the other at home that night. It sounds egalitarian in theory, but consider how it plays out in reality.

The most rotten day of Ross' career occurred on Black Monday when the stock market plummeted 500 points. Ross, a thirty-three-year-old financial planner, was inconsolable. When he arrived home that night, he was in no mood to do anything that smacked of domestic chores. Not that he was drained of energy—he had, if anything, a surplus of adrenaline. But rather than channeling it into tasks he sometimes shares with his wife—dusting, laundry, washing dishes, and feeding the family's two dogs—he opted instead to sputter and storm around the house in a Kabuki show of financial angst.

Fully aware of Ross' stress—how could she miss it?—Bridget snapped into action. "I thought my husband might jump out a window," says Bridget today, smiling at the recollection of his histrionics. "It has happened before in the brokerage industry."

To help her husband out, Bridget commandeered every aspect of the homefront. While encouraging Ross to share his anxieties and frustrations, she also straightened up the house, fed the dogs, cooked Ross a favorite dinner, and screened telephone calls—such as the ones from his mother, which she knew would only further fuel her husband's frenzy. After dinner, she ordered him into the car and took him to the movies. Her efforts, both nurturing and logistical, worked. By the end of the evening, Ross was feeling considerably calmer, even as Bridget found herself more than a little exhausted.

For Bridget, a reciprocal day of rottenness at work occurred recently when she made a presentation to an important client. Bridget, the thirty-three-year-old founder of a product-naming company, had spent weeks trying to create a perfect name for a new fast-food chicken sandwich. Throughout the process, her contacts with the restaurant chain had been very supportive of her efforts. But on the day of the final presentation, a high-ranking company officer she had never met before decided to drop in on the meeting. His off-the-cuff reaction to all her hard work: "I'm underwhelmed."

At home that night, Bridget was, by her own description, impatient, crabby, and sullen. And just as Ross had felt following his rotten day, she had no desire to deal with any of the additional stresses that come from attending to domestic duties. She opted to do only the bare minimum, that is, feed the hungry dogs and leave the rest of the homefront chores for another day.

When Ross arrived home an hour later, he could immediately see how upset his wife was. In his own way, he took pains to help her, encouraging her to talk about her frustrations and listening carefully to what she had to say. He even ran her a warm bubble bath so she could relax. But rather than using her soaking time to take up the slack on the domestic front—picking up the house, for instance, or making her a special dinner—he opted instead to pick up the phone. "The best thing I make," Ross concedes a tad sheepishly, "is dinner reservations."

Three Jobs, Two People

For millions of two-career couples across the nation, the experiences of the Mulligans and Hollanders are familiar variations on a recurrent theme. Stress—from overloads and conflicts at the office to seemingly endless domestic and child care duties at home—can seem inescapable and crushing. For many baby boom couples, life often devolves into an uneasy attempt to cram three full-time jobs onto the shoulders of two people—her career, his career, *plus* the myriad tasks once undertaken by their own fifties-era mothers.

Nolan Brohaugh, M.S.W., a senior associate of the Menninger Clinic, gives yearly seminars to executive couples on how to handle the tensions inherent to modern relationships. "One of the biggest problems we see in two-career couples," he explains, "is that no one is identified as the central nurturer, the caretaker of the relationship."

One frequent result, says Brohaugh, is nightly stress competitions with both partners jockeying at home for bragging rights to who had the worse day at the office. "What they're both really expressing in these discussions is an unmet need for nurturance," says Brohaugh. "They both want to prove they're the most stressed out so the other one will become the caretaker."

In more traditional family structures, this caretaker role (read "wife") was almost by definition stress-relieving for the wage-earning spouse, who ideally could come home every night to a domestic sanctuary: an orderly house, an organized social life, and great dollops of emotional support. Little wonder that working people of both genders so often long to have such a person back in their lives—who wouldn't find stress relief in the form of a full-time logistical expert/social secretary/personal psychologist?

Such a traditional arrangement allowed each spouse to concentrate their energies on one domain—an efficient, if sometimes stultifying, division of labor for at-home moms and workadaddies alike. For many two-career working couples, on the other hand, the line between home and work responsibilities is sometimes so blurry today that it can be fiendishly difficult to prevent overloads in one domain from contaminating the other.

No Parity When It Comes to Parties

Consider, for example, how hard it can be for a two-career couple to entertain friends after work. Says Kelly Joseph, twenty-seven, a marketer for children's camps: "I'll be at work and notice that it's getting late, and I've not had time to finish all the errands and prepare for dinner. So I'll call my husband, Jim, at his work and explain I'm running behind. I'll ask him to stop and pick up a few items. I am thinking I could use a little help, and it's really not much to ask him."

But Jim Joseph, twenty-seven, a manager for a pharmaceutical company, sees it a little differently. "Kelly will call," he says, "and drop this bomb on me. As soon as she hangs up, I'm thinking that I absolutely have to get the company's financials done by 6:00 P.M., I have dozens of sales calls to make, I'm way behind in everything else, and Kelly needs me to be home at five. I know she's not asking that much, but it really throws me off—I lose my concentration."

How exactly working couples are striving to reconfigure their relationships to make do without a traditional wife—or at least reapportion her stress-relieving tasks among the two of them—is a topic of keen interest to researchers. Armed with questionnaires and number-crunching computers capable of high level analysis, psychologists are just now beginning to tease out some of the subtle—and often surprising—ways that 1990s women and men are redefining their roles to deal with work and home stress.

To learn more, NYU researcher Niall Bolger, Ph.D., recently studied 166 married, working couples. "There is a lot of concern today," explains Bolger, "over the difficulties people have in modern marriages just balancing jobs and family life. Events in one area of your life can create problems in the other area of your life. We wanted to look at how bad events can set up subsequently bad events." Specifically, Bolger's study analyzed the flow of stress in two different directions: from home to work, and from work to home.

Home to Work

In the past, says researcher Bolger, many psychologists stereotypically assumed that domestic stress would be more likely to affect a woman's job performance than a man's. Bolger's data, however, showed precisely the opposite reaction. In all the socioeconomic groups he studied, women were able to keep stress at home from having a major impact on their job performance. Men, on the other hand, revealed an almost universal difficulty in leaving home problems at the office door.

"This finding definitely flies in the face of the idea that women will have more lost days or sloppy performance because of family problems," says Bolger. "The overall distress levels of women for the past thirty years have been relatively steady," he says, adding that in the past women have consistently reported higher levels of anxiety and depression than men. "Today, some studies often don't find *any* gender differences in distress. This isn't because women are becoming *less* distressed—it's because men are getting *more* distressed. Men are clearly having trouble handling problems at home, and it's affecting them in the workplace."

Consider one emblematic case in point. When their twelve-year-old daughter Bree came down with a fever one weekend, Kathy and Bob Johnson took her to their family doctor, who prescribed antibiotics for an ear infection. By Monday morning, Bree still had a fever, but her parents' interpretations of its significance varied widely.

Saleswoman Kathy opted to go on a scheduled sales call and keep in touch with Bree via car phone. Teacher Bob, whose school was only two blocks away from home, decided to get a substitute and stay home on Monday morning.

"I took things logically," says Kathy. "We had seen the physician and knew her problem was being treated. I also know Bree is a responsible person, who baby-sits for younger children. I knew she would take fluids and medication on her own and that I could check in by phone. I just had confidence that she would be all right by herself."

Bob says he admires his wife's calm logic but admits he can't always muster it for himself. "I worry, often foolishly, about freaky things happening to our kids," he says. "I tend to fantasize more about the negative aspects. Kathy is maybe more logically realistic." As Kathy had predicted, Bree's condition improved rapidly, eliminating Bob's need to stay home any longer from work.

Bolger speculates that one reason for pervasive male distress over home problems is that so many of the men in his study felt inadequate to shoulder their new responsibilities. "Most of the people in our sample were at least in their thirties," he explains, "and many men of that generation were not brought up to be skilled, comfortable, or used to doing lots of housework and child care. As a result, they may find it a lot harder to do. Whatever the reason, it was an empirical fact in the study: Men as a group are much more bothered by home overloads and things like child disciplinary problems than their wives are."

Another common source of home stress—marital arguments—also seems to affect men more at work the next day than women. Consider a typical fight, which was itself fueled in part by the husband's overload at work.

For a week before a medical malpractice trial, thirty-year-old attorney William Thompson worked fifteen hour days to get ready for litigation. When he came home exhausted one evening, his wife, Grace, twenty-eight, who writes insurance contracts for a large life insurance firm, sensed how grouchy he was the instant she mentioned her haircut.

"In his mind," Grace recalls, "William has all our money allocated. If I tell him I had an expense, like a haircut, which he didn't expect, he gets angry—especially if he's stressed out from work. Then I get mad because I feel I have the right to get my hair cut."

The skirmish quickly escalated into an argument, with William yelling and Grace eventually withdrawing into silence. The next day, the two headed off to work with the conflict still largely unresolved. As luck would have it, William had an unexpectedly easy day at the office—a fact that, he says, proved to be something of a curse.

"When something stressful is going on in my marriage, I *really* have a hard time concentrating on work," explains William. "It's especially bad when I have a run-of-the-mill day—then I don't have anything like a gun to my head to take my mind off the conflict at home."

For Grace, it's the opposite situation—her work, she says, provides a partial escape from home conflicts. "I can put it out of my mind to some extent," she says. "I think about the problem, but it's at the back of my mind."

Explanations vary for why females generally seem so much better at preventing the spillover of home stress into the workplace. Nancy Marshall, Ed.D., of the Wellesley College Center for Research on Women, speculates that Grace's "escape" theory may indeed be accurate. Because the majority of working women are still responsible for so much of the couple's domestic work, it makes sense that they would view their job as a kind of sanctuary. "Women," says Marshall, "have more to escape from than men."

Another factor, suggests Brohaugh, may be gender differences in soliciting and receiving social support. In one classic research study, women and men were asked to name their best friend. Women, nine times out of ten, named another woman. Men, on the other hand, usually named their wives. Similar studies have shown that women, on average, are able to derive emotional support from their friends as well as their husbands, whereas men tend to seek support exclusively from their wives. Marshall speculates that working women may well be tapping into a network of social support at work, and that men are choosing instead to keep home problems to themselves.

Anecdotal evidence for this hypothesis abounds. "When my husband and I fight," says Ann Swanson, thirty-eight, the manager of an upscale fabric store, "the people I feel close to at work will hear the story. I definitely talk about it at work, and that helps me blow off the episode. We have a nice social support system there."

Ann's husband, Robert, a thirty-eight-year-old corporate lawyer, says he also has good friends at work, "but they're not my best friends in the world." Robert admits he almost never discusses home problems with his colleagues.

Brohaugh suggests that men like Robert might well benefit from adopting their wives' broader network of emotional support. He urges men to confide their concerns to friends—a strategy that will not only help them better cope with stress, but often provides indirect benefits to their wives as well. "Men have traditionally over-relied on their wives to meet their emotional needs," Brohaugh explains. "This is another reason why tension levels are sometimes so high in two-career families."

Of course, understanding how home and work stress affect men and women differently is no excuse for preserving the household status quo. But it may help both genders see things better from the other's perspective, and, in fact, encourage both to give the other a little more slack during this time of generational change.

Work to Home

In the daily diaries that Niall Bolger's test subjects kept for six weeks, both women and men reported doing significantly less work than usual at home after a taxing day at work. But there were definite gender differences in how spouses reacted to their mates' need to cut back.

If the woman had an easy day and her husband didn't, Bolger found, she was very likely to "take up the slack" and assume some of his normal share of the domestic duties. In the process, she ended up reporting an overload of home stress each time her husband reported an overload of work stress. But when the opposite scenario occurred—that is, she had a bad day at work and he didn't—the man tended not to reciprocate with an extra effort on the homefront. He'd do his normal share of chores, but no more.

"If you ask almost any married woman, she'll say this description rings true," says Nancy Marshall. Though the most recent studies on domestic division of labor in working couples are starting to show some encouraging trends—men are slowly increasing their share of the load and women decreasing theirs—Marshall says that women still undertake significantly more of the burden than men.

"There are a lot of theories as to why this is the case," says Marshall, "but I think you can chalk it up to training." Many adults today, she says, were raised in households that emphasized a strong gender-based division of labor. "It can be hard to break that down because it threatens the sense of who you are as a man or woman."

Because of this, contend both Marshall and Brohaugh, domestic inequity is not a simple matter of oppressive males and long-suffering females. If it's true that many males have been trained in childhood to believe domestic chores are women's work, many females have been inculcated with the same message, one that can be surprisingly hard for both genders to shake.

Explains Brohaugh: "We operate on two different levels. There is the intellectual level that says, 'I understand that my marital relationship is different from my parents'—I not only accept this but I find it desirable.' Then there is the emotional level that says, 'This is different from what I learned, and what I learned was right.' When there is a struggle between intellect and emotion, emotion usually proves more powerful."

Witness how easily many working couples can be driven to distraction by snide comments from their own traditional parents. Recounts Brohaugh: "A man's father might say, 'Boy, she certainly has you henpecked,' or 'I can see who wears the pants in this family.' Or a mother will tell her daughter, 'You may be doing a super job at the office, dear, but your house is a mess.'"

The psychological momentum of early role modeling can make true domestic sharing an elusive goal. One theme that kept recurring after dozens of interviews with working couples is that pain over housework is rarely one-sided. To be sure, many of the women felt truly overwhelmed by the relentlessness of their second shift responsibilities. But there was also real suffering experienced by many of the men, who felt at once inept, incompetent, and besieged by wives whose housekeeping standards seemed too hopelessly high for them to ever meet—even when they tried in good faith to do so.

Sadly, many couples wait till such a breaking point before beginning to act. By the time they wind up in Brohaugh's office for help, he says, it's usually because inequity on the homefront has reached such a crisis that it has finally dawned on the man that there's a real chance he could lose his wife.

"Regardless of what men have learned as kids," says Bridget Hollander, "at some point, they have to accept the impact that their lack of helping out at home is having on the person they love. This was a devastating scenario early on in our marriage. I was doing about 99 percent of the work at home compared to Ross' 1 percent. But I have to give him credit—he's really made strides over the years. Let's put it this way—his mother would not recognize him today."

Ross concedes that his motivation to change has little to do with any inherent affection for housework. "Bridget is the most important person in my life," he says, "and it's important to me that nothing damages our relationship. Overburdening her was not good for us as a couple."

The Value of Emotional Caretaking: Understanding and Using Your Mate's Coping Style

As the Menninger Clinic's Nolan Brohaugh so poignantly noted, one of the most important—and missed—of a traditional homemaker's domestic job duties is the emotional nurturing of both her mate and children. Indeed, says Brohaugh, when working women joke, "What I need is a wife," they're expressing a need for more than just someone to wash the dishes—they are seeking the kind of personal, ongoing, emotional support that their own mothers typically provided to their fathers.

Working people today who strive for true domestic partnership need to know that each must, in a sense, be this kind of "wife" for the other. Not only is the providing of such emotional support just plain *kind,* it's also practical. By easing the tensions and jangled nerves that sap your partner's energy, you are making it much easier for him or her to function effectively at home in everything from child care to cleaning.

But as key as emotional caretaking is to balancing a relationship, it is not always an easy skill to master. Perhaps the most important key to effectively removing the burdens from your spouse's bowed shoulders is to realize that men and women, for the most part, tend to cope with their work stresses differently, says Bill Doherty, Ph.D., a professor of family social science at the University of Minnesota.

On the macro level, many men have been socialized to believe that their primary worth lies in career success and the money they bring home. "Grave threats to one's employment—such as being fired or failing to get a promotion—are clearly hard on both men and women," says Doherty. "But such threats seem to cut much more deeply in men." A variety of research studies on unemployment, says Doherty, are unequivocal: The impact of losing a job is much more devastating psychologically to men than women.

"A wife needs to know that any threat to her husband's career can be a real crisis of identity for him," says Doherty. "If she tries to help him cope by saying, 'Oh, well—there are other jobs,' she can miss the point of just how deeply it goes."

Even less drastic work stresses seem to bother men more than women. At home following a stressful day at work, the last thing many men want to do is talk about what's gone wrong.

Hank Yaeger, a school teacher who works with at-risk children, admits he's like this. "I *definitely* don't want to talk about the stresses of my job, because this often involves reliving some pretty sad stories. I would just as soon escape for a while, in some way or another, and not have to dwell on those particular cases."

"For many men," says Doherty, "an elaborate discussion of a negative work experience can feel like a reliving of that experience, and they wonder, 'For what purpose?'" Instead, men like Yaeger are more likely to use a variety of active and passive distractions to avoid thinking about the day. Some distractions, such as playing sports, puttering around in a garage workshop, or reading the newspaper for an hour or two, are benign. Others, however, are less so. As a group, says Doherty, men are much more likely than women to overindulge in alcohol as a means of coping with work stress.

They are also more likely to zone out in front of the TV for hours on end—possibly in an unconscious attempt to interrupt what one researcher has called the "stress-rehearsal process." According to John Condry, Ph.D., author of *The Psychology of Television*, a man who has an argument with his boss tends to relive it over and over again in his mind. TV, however, can effectively short-circuit this mental cycle. It's conceivable, at least, that male couch potatoes are really just self-medicating for stress.

Women who have suffered stress at work are much more likely to take an opposite approach to coping. Instead of distracting themselves from the experience, says Doherty, they often want to discuss the situation thoroughly, to analyze it from a variety of angles, and generally process verbally what's happened to them.

Hank's wife, Helen Yaeger, a bookseller, says that unlike her husband, she enjoys talking about her job—both its ups and its downs. "It's really important to me to talk about my work to Hank. Part of it is that I want a sounding board for my ideas, and I really admire Hank's ability to read people and advise me. Sometimes I just want to be reassured that I've made the right decisions, and I'm doing the right thing."

There are many exceptions to the patterns that the Yaegers illustrate, Doherty concedes. "But even when couples start off with both of them closer to the middle," he says, "there is a natural process of polarization that occurs in many marriages, so that small differences tend to get magnified."

One reason for this polarization is that many couples end up practicing a kind of maladaptive version of the golden rule—they try to help each other cope by providing the kind of emotional support they themselves would want. "Men often really think they are doing their wives a favor by encouraging them not to indulge in what they perceive as negative talk," says Doherty. "A husband often needs to realize that this is how his wife feels better, not worse, about work stress, and that he is doing her a favor to actually listen more."

Women, on the other hand, need to avoid making the opposite error, that is, trying to help their husbands by pushing them to communicate their feelings before they are ready to. "One big mistake that many wives make," says Doherty, "is that they not only try to force their husbands to talk, but they also try to arrange these talks according to *their* own timing, *their* own agenda. They want their husbands to talk now. But a lot of men feel they need to get their feelings under control *before* they can talk about it. Wives need to respect that."

In the couples he counsels, Doherty first attempts to get men and women to acknowledge the validity—and pervasiveness—of these different coping styles. This alone, he says, can be very liberating. "Most people don't realize that the differences they have in coping with stress are garden variety problems that many, many couples have," says Doherty. "Instead, they attribute these differences too much to the personality of their spouse or to some kind of flaw in their relationship." But once couples understand that there is no right or wrong way to cope with work stress, they are much less likely to personalize the other's behavior.

The second step, says Doherty, then becomes providing your partner with the kind of emotional support he or she actually wants—not the kind that you would necessarily want in his or her place. If a husband comes home upset from his job, says Doherty, "maybe the best thing his wife can do is to bring him a cup of coffee and just sit with him—and not make him feel he has to talk. If he's not forced into it, he may actually want to open up a little more later."

Doherty adds that a husband's need to zone out is not unlimited. "If a man wants his wife to be a full partner in their relationship," he says, "she *needs* to be able to take his emotional temperature." Doherty advises a stoical husband to provide his wife with a basic outline of what has happened to make him upset.

Men, on the other hand, can often best help women by encouraging them to confide work problems—and by giving them a period of full attention in which to do so. "A lot of men think their wives will talk for four hours about their work stress," says Doherty. "Most of the time, all she really needs is five or ten minutes of full, concentrated support, and that will free up the rest of the evening."

Doherty stresses that husbands should strive to listen and resist the urge to immediately begin problem solving. "It's important to let the other person talk for a while," says Doherty. "You don't have to say anything. Often later, people will be open to suggestions—but only after they've had a chance to ventilate for a while."

Getting in the Mood: Other Strategies to Keep Work Stress from Hindering Home Performance

To be sure, you won't always be able to completely leave job stresses behind at the office. But experts suggest that achieving at least a partial psychological separation between the two domains can put you in a better frame of mind to function effectively at home. For the traditional breadwinners of yesteryear, home was a passive sanctuary from the rat race, a place to be pampered and renewed. Home can still be such a sanctuary, albeit a much less passive one. Instead of losing yourself in an easy chair with the afternoon newspaper and a martini, you can rejuvenate your spirit by preparing a fine meal to the accompaniment of classical music or by restoring order to a cluttered room or by playing with your kids, in whose eyes you will always be number one. But in order for any of these household activities to be restorative, you're going to have to give them your full attention—and leave as much of your work woe behind as possible. Psychologists have found the following measures particularly helpful:

- *Try creating a buffer zone between work and home.* "A lot of people these days try and get in some exercise at the end of their working day," says Bolger. "A buffer could also be a short nap or reading a book—anything that clears your head and creates a psychological barrier between one domain and the other. This is one key to preventing stress spillover."

"I swim after work," says attorney William Thompson, "and it definitely helps diminish stress. By the end of a good workout, I have all but forgotten what I was so tense about less than forty-five minutes earlier." When William arrives home after swimming, adds his wife, Grace, he's not only much less likely to take a bad day out on her, he's also much more likely to tackle his share of the home duties, thanks to the break he's had.

- *Try not to misinterpret the source of your partner's stress.* Most people often blame themselves first, even when the problem has nothing to do with them. "Discounting is a good word," says Bolger. "If you know your spouse has had a bad day at work, you won't interpret it as something you did, and that can go a long way in preventing you from getting upset and arguments from developing."

- *If you know you aren't to blame for your partner's mood, tread lightly when you sense your mate is upset.* For some couples, a little temporary separation inside the home can go a long way to defuse tensions. "I know when to look at Helen and when not to," says Hank Yaeger. "There are times when I definitely won't gaze into her eyes— she's like Medusa; I'll turn to stone. When you see venom there, you have to decide if you can help—and if you know you can't, you have to save yourself."

On such occasions, Hank admits that he "moseys off" to another part of the house, where he usually tackles a household chore like putting away laundry. It's a bifold strategy both he and Helen concede has helped prevent more than a few unnecessary arguments. Not only does the separation given Helen time to work through her feelings by herself, but once she's feeling better, her husband's contribution to the home-front makes her feel even better.

Why Male "Helping" Is Not Enough

All right. Let's assume you have taken to heart your mate's work stress—and done your best to help him cope with it in the way that he prefers to cope. Everything's copacetic, right? Except for the fact that your kids need dinner, your floors need to be vacuumed, and there's so much dirty laundry in your basement you have to swim through underwear to get to the washer. It's time to tackle the physical workload, and the man in the relationship is now ready to . . . *help*.

If there is one word that makes working women cringe, it's probably this one: *Help*. As in—"Let me *help* with the chores, honey."

To most of us fellows, such a comment merely epitomizes our nice-guy, decent natures. But to many women, what they really hear is this: "We both know these chores are your ultimate responsibility, dear, but if you spell out exactly what you want me to do, I will—begrudgingly—*help* you with your work. And, by the way, you better show me some appreciation for my *help*. And if you want me to *help* again, you will have to remind me each and every single occasion this obnoxious task comes up."

Sound far-fetched? Recent studies have actually shown that significant numbers of men are becoming increasingly passive-aggressive as women become more and more self-assertive. "It's true," one husband confided to me when his wife was out of earshot. "When my wife asks me to do something around the house, I always tell her, 'Sure, I'd be glad to.' But even as I'm mouthing these words, I know in my own mind I'm probably *not* going to do it, at least in this lifetime. The truth is, she nags me—and this is my way of refusing to submit to her nagging."

Even families who are committed to egalitarianism at home often live out this scenario. Jim Joseph, for instance, says he frequently assists at home, but he is notoriously slow to initiate action. "Jim will pretty much help but I always have to ask him," says his wife, Kelly. "I have to write down a list of what he should do, otherwise something else might come up and it won't get done."

"What can I say?" Jim shrugs sheepishly. "I guess she's right."

Men, of course, are not the only ones whose passive-aggressive behavior is likely to trigger nagging. As many parents of teenagers come to understand, the amount of work an average teen undertakes to get out of work can be prodigious. The mother of a famous Minnesota politician once related to me the difference in work-shirking styles of her two sons. Son A, not the politician, would balk like clockwork every time she demanded he take out the garbage. "I won't do it," he'd say. "And you can't make me!" Maybe she couldn't, but when the lad's father arrived home from work and the garbage was still sitting in the kitchen, he would literally pick Son A up along with the garbage and escort them both out to the curb.

Son B, on the other hand, never balked. Instead, he would always immediately agree to do the job. "He'd tell me, 'Mom, I would be so happy to take out the garbage for you. It's an honor to be asked!'" the mother recalls. "But then he'd slink off to his room and forget about it. The net result was that he *never* once actually took out the garbage, and we never ended up making him. I think that's when I first knew he would be successful in politics."

Why Female Autocracy Is Self-Defeating

But men (and politically minded teenagers)—though arguably needing to make the *greater* change in their approach to household work—are not the only ones who need to change their attitudes and behavior. Women who feel burdened by being responsible for most household matters might want to ask themselves these questions:

- When your mate is taking care of the kids, do you find yourself frequently "checking" on him to make sure he's not somehow screwing up?

- When he is cleaning, do you hover over him like a supervisor, making suggestions or criticizing his work?

- Do you have trouble surrendering control of the household management?

Frank Sinatra may have catapulted "My Way" into something of an American anthem, but when it comes to sharing household chores, a "My Way" autocrat is far more likely to beget resentment than to get results. No one—man, woman, child, or teen—likes to be nagged and nitpicked. And indeed, when one partner is too quick to criticize another's attempts to share responsibility at home ("Idiot! You folded the towels all wrong!"), you have a situation tailor-made to insure many so-called slackers won't even try.

"There are couples in which the woman can be a real taskmaster," acknowledges psychotherapist Gail Hartman. "It's as if she owns the business of the family, and one of her subordinates is her husband. Damn it, she is ticked at him because he won't own the business with her. And yet she won't sell him any shares."

According to sociologist Arlie Hochschild, there are several reasons for household control-freakiness in some women. For one thing, there can occasionally be legitimate concerns, based on his lack of experience, about a husband's child-rearing abilities. Hochschild recommends that when this is truly a problem, husbands and wives take a parenting class together until the wife feels confident that her husband can handle child-care duties competently.

Another—and arguably much more common—reason is a woman's own ambivalence about her identity at home and work. Many women, experts suggest, are as wedded to their domestic role as men are to a lack of one. Though such women say they want their husbands to share responsibility, on another level they are anxious about surrendering the power that comes from being in charge.

Indeed, in some cases, women who feel they have no control over their situation at work can be particularly hesitant to give up being boss at home. It's not unheard of for such wives to treat their husbands like misbehaving children. Such treatment has a way of becoming a self-fulfilling prophecy.

Hochschild also found that for a subset of working women, what they really wanted was *not* an equal distribution of household work, but rather greater recognition and appreciation for the work they were doing. As Natalie put it, a little thanks can go a long way.

Many women, however, truly do want a more equal distribution of responsibility. And for that to happen, it's critical that they have reasonable expectations of their mates and children. "A woman can't expect to clone herself in her husband," explains psychotherapist Hartman. "That is a sure road to disappointment." Rather, other family members should be allowed to do a job in their own way—provided it's executed with reasonable competence.

Ah ha! snap many women at this point. *But they never do it reasonably right.*

Dirt Blindness

Take dirt, for example. Many women are very quick to comment on their husbands' or children's abysmal standards of cleanliness. This has reached the status of a cliché: *Men don't see dirt.* In the executive couples he counsels, says Brohaugh, the wife often complains that even when her husband does clean around the house, she has to re-clean. "Men are just as capable of seeing dirt as women," says Brohaugh. "They just have to practice it."

There's also a practical component here that needs to be addressed. Oftentimes, says Brohaugh, men have not ever been taught how to do common chores, from ironing to dusting. Women, who frequently have learned these skills early on, assume that they come naturally to everyone, which is not the case. Once men have been shown how to do a given chore, they feel more competent at undertaking it—and less likely to come up with excuses.

On the other hand, Brohaugh and an increasing number of marriage and family therapists believe that heightened male participation is only a partial solution to home overloads. "Men do need to learn to do more around the house," agrees Diane Sollee, M.S.W., former program director for the Washington, D.C.–based American Association for Marriage and Family Therapy. "But it's also true that women need to learn how to let go of some of those tasks."

"Women can learn something from their husbands' frequent *disregard* for cleanliness," Brohaugh says. "The floor does not have to be clean enough to eat off of if you have a table. It may be that the kitchen floor gets washed every other week instead of every week. No one will die from it. Which is better? To tolerate somewhat lower standards of housecleaning, or to live with a high degree of stress in your life?"

This shift downward from perfect standards is also a critical component in allowing children to become responsible and contributing members of the household. A seven year old, for example, can definitely learn to make a bed. But if your idea of what constitutes a properly made bed includes hospital corners so tightly tucked that you can bounce a dime a full yard off the sheets, chances are most seven year olds are going to have problems measuring up. Kids definitely need to learn household skills from bed-making to cooking, but these are skills that require practice.

You have a choice in which messages you send your children. On the one hand, you can demand perfection and tell them that if they can't do it up to your standards, don't even bother trying. On the other hand, you can instill a critical value that responsibilities at home are shared by all who live there—and make them feel good about the contributions they can make.

A Hard Change Coming

Anthropologist Margaret Mead once suggested that it takes a full generation for cultural attitudes to change. Working couples in the 1990s—the sons and daughters of a different approach to marriage—may one day prove to be the vanguard of an enduring social arrangement.

"I am *hoping* the changes that our generation has seen will continue," says researcher Marshall. "Sometimes there is enough of a backlash that I wonder if we'll see two steps forward and one back."

For their part, Kelly and Jim Joseph say they are both ready to take that backward step. "In a couple of years, Kelly will leave her job and devote her time to raising our family," says Jim, who admits he's looking forward to the traditional division of labor he grew up with.

"We both agreed before we got married," says Kelly, "that I would work until we had kids, then I'd stay home. I don't think I am alone in thinking that raising a family is the most important job I can do. The majority of my female friends, who are very successful in their careers, have all told me that this is what they would most like to do if they could."

But other two-career couples say they can't conceive of turning back the clock. "I'm convinced this is a permanent change for women and men alike," says Bridget Hollander, who says she and her husband have both thrived as their two-career marriage has evolved over the past nine years. "We're pioneers in a whole new way of life, and there's a natural stress that comes from forging new ground. But Ross and I have every confidence we will triumph together. We're committed to making new rules that are fair and work for us, and to creating out of our marriage a haven from the stresses we have chosen to live out in the workplace."

It's a commitment that many couples share. In the next chapter, we will also see how hard it can be to fulfill.

 ANATOMY OF CHANGING HEARTS
How to Reach a Lasting Accord

If a house be divided against itself, that house cannot stand.
—The Gospel According to St. Mark

Domestic happiness, thou only bliss of paradise that has survived the fall!
—William Cowper

Are tectonic plates dishwasher-safe?
—Herb Caen, *San Francisco Chronicle*, 8/12/93

If you have an important point to make, don't try to be subtle or clever. Use a pile driver. Hit the point once. Then come back and hit it again. Then hit it a third time—a tremendous whack.
—Winston Churchill

At our wedding ceremony, the minister made the observation that "some people need to learn that discipline and diligence are important, while others need to learn that it is equally important to learn to relax and enjoy your time together." There was an audible giggle from both sides of the aisles when she said that.
—Patricia M.

Delores' Story

"How did we divide up domestic work? The simple—and pathetic—answer is that we didn't. If something needed to be done, I did it. In the last decade of the twentieth century, we had the kind of domestic arrangement which would have looked familiar to women at the dawn of civilization—except that I, too, held down a full-time job outside the house. With the clarity of 20/20 hindsight, I can now see a virtual road map leading from the early days of our courtship to my eventual frustration, annoyance, exhaustion, and finally rejection of our domestic situation.

"At my insistence, we did not share living quarters until we were married—the idea being we could keep our lives more independent. In reality, he was soon spending every night at my place and using his own apartment as a workspace. He felt no need to help out with domestic chores at 'my place' "—he never once cleaned, took out the garbage, or went grocery shopping.

"He also had tremendous tolerance for dirt and clutter. When I asked him, for instance, to be tidier with his clothes, he'd say *he* had no problem with clothing strewn about. If I had a problem with it, then I could pick the stuff up. Is this passive-aggressive or what?

"I think he had a root belief, which was never explored on either of our parts for many years, that these chores were truly women's work. Whatever the reasons, our patterns of household division of labor started early and did not change much after we were married.

"Consider a small example of how my husband avoided responsibility at all costs. I would always ask him to buy the toiletries *he* needed—shaving cream, lotion, razors, and the like. He never did. Instead, he'd use the same razor for a month if I let him. It wasn't because he was cheap—he would just rather 'make do' than remember to replace the item. In the end, it almost always came down to me replacing the stuff.

"Then one day after an argument about this, he came home with a shopping bag full of creams, potions, and pastes. He threw the bag down with a huff and said, 'There! Are you happy now?' He completely missed the point, choosing to grandstand instead. Standing there with his big bag full of stuff, he worked himself into a righteous fit rather than act like an adult and take responsibility for his own basic needs.

"A story like this seems ridiculous, but the mundane chore stuff surrounds you twenty-four hours a day, and, when it festers, it can really grind away your quality of life. By the end, our different expectations for how our home should be run had become completely incompatible. (Note: Delores and her husband are now divorced; he was unavailable for comment.)

"Writing this down has been a rather emotional experience for me—dredging up all that petty, nerve-wracking bullshit and seeing how it still hits all the same hot buttons. The situation was never adequately dealt with at the time, never resolved, never markedly changed or improved. So thinking about it now is like pressing a rewind button and reliving the same aggravations and regretting all over again that the situation wasn't rectified.

"In retrospect, it becomes increasingly apparent to me that my ex-husband's unwillingness to 'get with the program' was probably his way of acting out in response to whatever disappointments or frustrations he might have felt with our relationship. He had no physical or intellectual handicaps that would have prevented him from doing this stuff, yet he never assumed any responsibility for our basic domestic needs. Maybe we could have improved the inequitable distribution of chores. But it would have required a lot of time, patience, dedication, and rethinking of very well-entrenched habits. By the time our chore wars came to a head, the last thing I wanted to do was start rebuilding from the ground up."

Mending a Mangled Marriage

It's probably impossible to estimate how many women like Delores will see their marriages end bitterly in large part because of the unfairness of the home work situation. For every such divorce, there are no doubt countless other unhappy couples, their relationship on some level poisoned by this issue.

The marriage therapists I interviewed all agreed that chores inequity may not be the first reason couples *cite* as the cause for their seeking help. But it's a topic that *always* surfaces during therapy, one that invariably stirs the enmities and passions of both individuals.

To better understand how the chore wars can get so bad that they split families apart, I conducted in-depth interviews with several couples who came to within a hair's width of divorcing. This point came only after years of fighting chore wars, years that had left each partner chronically depressed—the women from overwork, the men from their partners' constant recriminations. Only by successfully resolving domestic work and child-care issues were they able to save their relationships.

But save them they did. And they graciously agreed to tolerate my many questions about the process—an incredible act of generosity, given how intrusive these questions were into some of the most painful and intimate aspects of their union. They agreed in the hope that their own stories might help other couples avoid letting the chore wars progress to the point of domestic Armageddon.

Reading these stories may strike painful nerves of recognition. But know, too, that both these stories have decidedly happy endings. No matter how bad things were when they sought help, each couple succeeded in salvaging their relationship with the help of an objective therapist who helped them recognize, untangle, and reframe attitudes and behaviors that had made them both miserable for years.

The fact that couples *in extremis* succeeded so well proves that this problem is *not* intractable. Take heart—no matter how bitter the fighting has become in your own chore wars, you can reach an armistice. And for couples willing to make the effort, your relationship can become better than you may now imagine possible.

Such was definitely the case with two Pittsburgh lawyers who lost—but refound—their love for each other.

Litigators in Love

They met poolside on a fine late spring afternoon in Pittsburgh. For weeks, Francesca, twenty-five, had been studying feverishly for her bar exam, but on this day she'd carried her reams of case studies to a table outside so that her body, if not her mind, could get some fresh air and sunshine.

Dirk, twenty-seven and already a practicing litigator, was playing a spirited game of singles on the apartment complex's adjacent tennis court. Though his central vision was focused on his buddy's serve, Dirk's peripheral vision unerringly zeroed in on the attractive blonde with the hyperserious expression. When a sudden gust blew her papers off the table, he yelled "Hold it!" to his buddy, dropped his racquet, and chased down the fugitive torts.

"Here you go," he said, smiling as he handed Francesca her papers in a neat stack.

Fast-forward fourteen years, and Dirk and Francesca are happily married today with two great kids and successful law careers. In retrospect, their meeting by the pool almost seemed like a happy domestic omen: Dirk, the modern man, chasing down scattered papers and restoring order from chaos for Francesca, the career-focused modern woman. But from this propitious meeting to their current marital bliss, the path was anything but straightforward. A marriage therapist would later tell them that the only reason she agreed to counsel them at all was to keep them from making "mincemeat" out of each other during what she believed was certain divorce.

"Mincemeat—that was the actual word she used," says Francesca. "She figured we were hopeless, and all she was hoping to do was keep us from destroying each other and our first child."

Over her pinstripe corporate lawyer uniform, Francesca is wearing a fuchsia apron studded with rhinestones and words printed with a magic marker by six-year-old daughter, Char: I LOVE YOU, MOM. "When you think back on it, our first meeting was kind of an omen," she continues, while scooping kibble into the family Akita's bowl. "But the omen *wasn't* Dirk restoring order to disorder," says Francesca with a laugh. "It was more like this: I was working. He was playing."

Across the kitchen table, cloaked in a tennis shirt, khaki shorts, and a purple rhinestone-studded I LOVE YOU, DAD apron of his own, Dirk shrugs sheepishly. "I admit it," he says. "I was extremely uninformed and insensitive. My life had to change, and, looking back on it now, I realize I was completely unprepared for the responsibilities and coming changes of family life. That's definitely a part of my past I take no pride in today."

To be sure, domestic discord did not descend upon Dirk and Francesca overnight. As is the case with so many couples who start out with egalitarian intentions, unfairness crept up upon them so gradually they could hardly sense the growing threat to their marriage. Here's how it happened.

Six months after their initial poolside meeting, Dirk and Francesca became engaged and moved in together. Before this joining of households, each had inhabited a small apartment and lived on their own without noticeable problems. There were some minor differences: Francesca's apartment was *very* neat and clean—and Dirk's was marginally less so. They both did their own laundry and cooked for themselves. If anything, Dirk's prowess in the kitchen surpassed that of his fiancée.

"It really surprised me," says Francesca. "He would cook these entire family meals just for himself—you know, chicken or fish with some vegetables and a potato side dish and a salad. My idea of dinner tended more toward yogurt, pizza, or the free hors d'oeuvres at happy hour."

When they began sharing a two bedroom apartment, each naturally gravitated to his or her area of strength. Dirk did all the food-related chores: planning meals, shopping for groceries, cooking, and cleaning the dishes afterward. Francesca handled laundry and housecleaning. Apartment living meant there were no outside chores to do—no mowing, for instance, or snow shoveling. All in all, the workload was easy to handle, and they never argued about chores allocation, never even thought about it.

Almost exactly one year after they first met, they married. For the next two years, they continued to live harmoniously in their apartment. Indeed, everything was going along swimmingly—but the water was about to turn treacherous.

Lovers in Litigation

Looking back on the early years of their marriage, the two say they can remember only minor vignettes that might have served as red flags for the future. Driving to their downtown law offices one morning, for example, Francesca mentioned it might be nice to get a second car, a new one. "New car?" Dirk snapped. "If we get one, you know who'll be driving this clunker."

Such occasional episodes notwithstanding, Dirk truly thought of himself as a liberal guy, a feminist even. What he didn't realize was just how much his own father's attitudes had shaped his emotional core—and how powerful this role modeling would prove. "My father would go to work every day and earn an income," Dirk recalls. "This was his job. And he would tell my mother, 'Hey, the house, the kids—they're your responsibility.' "

Until Francesca got pregnant, the two enjoyed a habitual routine—he would work from 9:00 A.M. to 6:00 P.M., then go to the local gym for three hours of R&R. She would work from 8:00 A.M. to 9:00 P.M., then they'd rendezvous at home where Dirk would cook them both a nice dinner.

Throughout her pregnancy, Dirk continued his daily pattern as if nothing had changed. He didn't become a doting father-to-be, nor did he become mean and jealous of the unborn child. *He just didn't change— at all.*

"It never even registered to me that our whole world was changing," he says today. "I was unsentimental and detached about the whole thing. Looking back, I think maybe I was threatened by change. I really am a creature of habit, and I think I just shut the pregnancy out of my mind and acted as if nothing was going to happen."

Francesca, for her part, was not exactly hurt by her husband's indifferent attitude. Nor did she give his detachment much thought at the time. "I didn't really question it," she says today. "I found myself approaching motherhood in a very traditional way. I just assumed it was my job to be pregnant, my job to take over this aspect of our lives."

By the time their son, Alec, was born, the two had not once discussed how much their lives would be impacted by parenthood. Once Alec arrived, however, Francesca found herself making major accommodations. "I was in charge of finding suitable day care," she says. "I also knew what the baby needed in terms of food, so I took over much of what had been Dirk's responsibility—shopping and cooking meals. There was never any question which one of us would reduce hours at work—I cut back to two-thirds time, and Dirk continued as if nothing had happened."

Francesca says that it was hard to pinpoint when her resentment began to swell. An extremely energetic and focused woman, her personality was such that she would do everything she felt needed to be done, provided there were enough hours in the day. She was Supermom, a woman who found herself often brewing a pot of coffee at midnight so she could work two or three hours when her baby and husband were fast asleep and their household was quiet. Soon she was averaging four or five hours of sleep—if that—each night.

Her emotions, she acknowledges about this period in her life, were decidedly complex. "I went along feeling on some level that my life with my husband had become so unfair. But on the other hand, there were things I just didn't want him to do. Parenting was my turf; I wanted it done my way. I didn't want to give up any control."

Like tectonic plates grinding together beneath an apparently calm surface, unseen pressures were starting to build. Still, the two continued to avoid any discussion of what was going on; they never even acknowledged something was not right. Francesca found herself quietly seething—anger that was all the more difficult for her to tolerate because she knew, on some level, she was enabling, maybe even encouraging, Dirk's irresponsibility.

For his part, Dirk felt that his wife had somehow lost all capacity to have fun in life. He resented her smoldering resentment; he came to view her as a chronic kill-joy. Their mutual resentments and anger begot more ill feelings. Their sex life stopped. More and more, Dirk sought joyfulness not from his marriage but from his buddies.

It was against this backdrop of their deteriorating relationship that he talked his wife into moving back to a small town outside Pittsburgh where he had grown up. "It's a perfect place to raise children," he told her.

"I agreed to the move," she says, "but I was very conflicted about it. This was completely Dirk's agenda—I was subordinate all the way." Suddenly, Francesca found herself in charge of a much larger house set in a community where she knew no one. And into her already impossible schedule of work and mothering, she now needed to add an extra hour and a half of commuting time back and forth from her law firm.

For Dirk, life still hadn't changed much, except that now he was happier than ever having a bunch of his hometown friends to goof off with. And here, in the same town he himself had been raised in, the lessons of Dirk's father seemed even more impossible to ignore. Hey, take 'em. They're your kids. "Things became unbearable," says Francesca. "My resentment was so high now it was bound to burst."

Armageddon

On one overcast Saturday morning in November, Dirk was preparing to leave, as always, to go to the gym for his three-hour weekend workout. Before he could leave the house, however, Francesca asked him, if he would promise to be home by noon. She had arranged to go out to lunch and then shopping with her first girlfriend in their new town. She didn't ask her husband to come home *earlier* than usual—just to make sure he arrived at his customary time. Only if he would "baby-sit" their infant son could she keep her lunch date.

Dirk promised he'd come straight home. But at noon, there was no sign of him. Nor did he arrive at 1:00 P.M. In fact, it wasn't until 2:30 that he finally did show.

"Where have you been?" Francesca asked him, furious at his lack of consideration.

"I decided to grab some lunch," he explained. "Then I stopped to get the car washed."

As angry as Francesca was, Dirk was upset, too. What he didn't tell his wife was what he was really thinking: *She has no right to control my life. I'll get home when I want to.*

"Thinking back on it," Dirk says today, "by the time we hit that point in our marriage, there was so much anger and bitterness that I think I was doing things like this on purpose, as a way of showing my own anger. I knew we were both unhappy. It was obvious that she was overworked and at her wit's end, and it was obvious I was not helping. It never even occurred to me to think, 'Well, she's doing ten chores, and I'm doing minus three—maybe we should shift the work allocation.' Instead, my thoughts about a solution—and this will show you how little of a clue I actually had—were that everything would be a lot happier if she would just 'lighten up.' I truly did not comprehend what a jerk I was being."

By this point, the two had not only stopped having sex, they had pretty much stopped even conversing. Minutes after Dirk's belated arrival that Saturday afternoon, Francesca got in the car and headed for her friend's house. Halfway there, she spotted a phone booth. She stopped the car, called her husband, and told him, "I think we should get a divorce."

Playing the divorce card wasn't a last-ditch gambit to shock Dirk into change. In her own mind, Francesca had come to truly believe she'd be better off without him. "This sounds terrible," she says, "but I was thinking to myself, 'What do I need him for?' I was doing everything; he was doing nothing. All he was doing was making me miserable."

Dirk, for his part, was so unmoved by her words that to this day he cannot even remember the details of their conversation. "I knew our marriage had turned ugly—this was not a shock or a surprise to me. If anything, I kind of wanted a divorce myself."

The writer G. K. Chesterton once observed that "The way to love anything is to realize it might be lost." In the next couple days, Dirk found himself face-to-face with just how much he still loved his wife. It did not take him long to realize how much he wanted to save his marriage, to set things right. He asked her if she would consider going to a marriage counselor, but she said no—too much damage had already occurred. But he continued to argue for one last chance, saying that they owed that much to each other and to their now eighteen-month-old son, Alec. Eventually, Francesca relented, though she told herself she was only doing it in the hopes the counselor could make their split more amicable.

Dirk was now desperate to make the marriage work again. He was also desperately confused as to how things could ever have gotten so bad. "When I started in therapy," he says, "I felt like—this is the only way I can describe it—I was in a jungle. I felt like I had no idea how I had gotten there. I felt somebody just dropped me in the middle of the jungle, and, until I met my therapist, I didn't know how to get the hell out. And all of a sudden our therapist, one step at a time, started showing me, 'Hey, here is the path. Here is the way this started. Don't you see that here is the way you got to there, and here is the path out of there?' It was like, slowly, with a machete, I was able to start cutting down some of the vines and let the light in. I started to understand how I had gotten into this predicament, and to honestly appreciate how Francesca felt about what had happened for years. It took me a long time, but I did come to grips with the fact that I had really not made any effort to see things from Francesca's point of view."

The therapy continued once a week for nearly a year. Sometimes the couple would see the therapist together; sometimes she would schedule individual appointments. In hindsight, the complementary changes each spouse underwent seem straightforward enough, perhaps even self-evident. But to loved ones *in extremis,* understanding the obvious in an intellectual way is a far cry from living it emotionally.

It took Dirk, for instance, many sessions before it truly dawned on him that the unfairness of the domestic workload was really a root problem. This had never been an issue with his own parents—how could it be such a big deal in his own life? "My mother worked part-time," he says, "but she never let that get in the way of doing everything at home, from raising the kids to performing all aspects of household work. My father's idea of pitching in was to make a cup of tea when he was finished eating dinner."

Francesca, too, found herself needing to jettison some of her own attitudes about household roles. "Part of me believed deep down that this was my work to handle alone," she says. "But what both Dirk and I neglected to factor in was that I, like Dirk, also had a full-time job away from home."

In the beginning, both spouses needed to overcome deep-seated resentments and work together toward a common solution. For Dirk, this meant learning that his life could not remain untouched by fatherhood, that he would have to learn to adapt and shoulder significant new responsibilities. He would, in short, have to become a major contributor to the household they all shared. For Francesca, it meant giving her husband a chance to make this change. She would have to keep an open mind and believe at least in the theoretical possibility he could make such a change, even though she had never seen the slightest evidence for it in the past. She would, in short, have to learn to trust her husband again, trust that he truly would honor his commitments. Only such trust could hope to supplant the dark emotions built up over the years.

One of the first assignments their therapist gave them was to make individual contracts with themselves that they would commit to hanging on to the marriage for one more month. These contracts were not between the two of them, but rather to themselves as individuals. Says Francesca: "She didn't make us promise to each other that we'd stay together, because obviously one of us would do something to piss the other off, and that would provide a reason to give up and say, 'Oh, well, forget it. You don't deserve it this month.'"

The therapist also convinced them to commit to go out on a date one night a week and do something enjoyable together. And she urged them to try, on a relatively small-step basis, to reconfigure the care of Alec. Recalls Dirk: "I made a commitment to give up going to the gym on Saturday mornings and instead stay home and take care of our son so Francesca could have some time by herself."

The first of these two commitments, that is, date night, occurred without a hitch, but the transfer—albeit limited—of parental control over Alec proved very difficult for Francesca. She did leave the house on Saturday mornings, but her time alone was hardly the relaxing experience she had fantasized it might be. Instead, she found herself anxious that her husband would somehow do something that might imperil Alec's well-being, or that he might fail to do something that might safeguard it.

For Dirk, his wife's lack of confidence in his fathering abilities was at once hurtful and understandable. "It could be horrible at times," he recalls. "I mean, I was really trying to make contributions, and the last thing I wanted was for Francesca to immediately say, 'Well, gee, you fed him, but this, this, and this weren't done right.' It was like I was doing it my way, and I felt that that should be well enough.

"Now, having said that, I have to also admit that there were two sides to this, too. Many of the times when Francesca criticized me, it was because I wasn't doing a perfect job—in fact, I wasn't doing it that well at all. But I think in fairness that I was starting from zero, and they do say practice makes perfect. It's like a kid—you have to go through this process where you let them make mistakes, and you tolerate the mistakes, because that is the only way they are going to improve."

Clearly, Dirk's mistakes were not imperiling the baby's welfare—even Francesca acknowledged that. "It was hard for me, but what it boiled down to is that I had to let Dirk have his own relationship with our son. And I needed to learn that he didn't have to feed Alec at the exact time I said he had to be fed, or feed him the exact amount I said. I had to let him find his own way."

"Eventually," says Dirk, "my wife gave me some margin of error, and over time I got better at a number of parenting skills."

After the first month, the two renewed their contracts for another month, then another, until they eventually went to a three-month contract. Describing change in overview may make it seem simple and straightforward, but in reality it was incremental, hard won, and subject to fits and starts. Still, the increments were by-and-large positive ones, and the two found themselves recommitted with each small success.

The better and more reliable Dirk became in terms of child care, the more Francesca was able to trust him to do a good job. During her Saturday mornings of freedom, her impulse to call to check on things at home diminished, and she found herself gradually able to relax and have fun. But Francesca was not the only one finding a new kind of pleasure in life. Dirk was quickly developing his own bond with Alec, a bond that had been all but impossible to form when his wife had assumed complete responsibility for the boy. Instead of feeling that he was missing out on his Saturday workouts to baby-sit their child, he began to enjoy staying home, indeed he looked forward to his exclusive father-and-son time, which he found both fun and more rewarding than he had imagined possible. Perhaps the greatest beneficiary of all was Alec himself, a keen-witted toddler who adored his father.

As the therapist continued to help Dirk learn how to assume more responsibility, and Francesca learn how to surrender enough control for Dirk to find room to operate, she also worked on their communication style. As lawyers, each spouse spent much of his or her day in extremely adversarial relationships. Dirk, a litigator, admitted he loved to fight in the courtroom. Francesca, a corporate attorney, also spent much of her professional life competing to win.

"These are great skills to have in a legal environment," says Dirk today, "but when you bring them home, you're really looking for trouble."

"Everything was win-win for him; I mean everything," says Francesca. "I am by nature not so innately confrontational myself, so when he would use his 'tear 'em apart' skills on me during the early years of our marriage, I would shut down and withdraw—I couldn't deal with him on that level."

Dirk admits he would actually pace the floors when he argued with his wife, almost as if were making a case before an unseen jury. "She would accuse me of giving her the third degree," says Dirk. "And she was absolutely right—I was cross-examining her. But I didn't know I was doing it."

During their group counseling sessions, Dirk would often slip into his Perry Mason style, and the therapist would catch him at it. " 'Right there,' she would say. 'You're doing it. See what you just did?' " Chuckling, Dirk says: "I was probably more oblivious than most people, so it really helped that she would point this out. I mean, it was like training a dog. You catch them in the act of doing a bad behavior, and it really leaves an impression."

Francesca knew that therapy was making headway when Dirk did not try to argue his way out of such occasions. "Instead, he would say, 'Whoa, jeez—you're right. This is a cross-examination.' And the less he did that to me, the less confrontational, he was and the more supportive he became, the more I felt I had a safe environment at home. I stopped withdrawing inside myself—I came out and started to interact with him again."

And Baby Makes Four

About halfway through their year of therapy, with many issues still unresolved, Francesca became pregnant. "I think at the time we were still not very close," she says, "and in some regards, you could say that when parents are having problems, it's the worst time to have a child. We didn't intend for this to happen, but the fact it did really renewed our commitment to try and make this marriage work."

The therapist suggested they could use the pregnancy to really work on many of the issues that had for so long plagued their marriage. Dirk, who had been so emotionally distant during his wife's first pregnancy, found himself acting completely differently this time. "He tried very, very hard to be supportive, empathetic, and devoted," says Francesca. "It was very nice situation for me."

"The irony is that she says he *tried* very hard to be supportive," adds Dirk. "But the fact was that by this point, I *felt* so involved that being supportive wasn't an effort at all. I was a different person than I was the first time around."

To their mutual astonishment, both spouses found themselves falling in love with each other all over again. When Charlotte was born late that year, she came into the world with two doting parents, not to mention a thrilled older brother.

Six years later, the family continues to do great. "I can't tell you how happy I am," says Francesca. "Dirk is an absolutely terrific father, and the two of us have transformed our marriage into a great working partnership. From our therapist's point of view, we were her great success story—though we certainly weren't an overnight success story. It took a lot of work, and you know, we continue to build on it to this day."

"I truly feel that therapy saved my life," adds Dirk. "Knock on wood, but our relapses have been very minor, and we're both more than willing to go back for a 'tune-up' if we find we need it. But so far, we've been able to solve any problems on our own by talking things over and coming up with a solution we both agree on." As a final added bonus, the couple says, they've found that many of the same skills that helped get them back on track are also working in terms helping their growing children learn responsibility at home. "We're confident," says Dirk, "that chore wars won't cause the same problems in their future relationships that we experienced in our marriage."

Working with a Safety Net

Since triumphing over their own problems, Dirk and Francesca have been surprised by how many of their friends have suffered similar discord on the homefront. In one two-lawyer household, the man actually gave up his career to become a full-time, stay-at-home father, an arrangement that seems to suit both spouses well. Some gay friends who share a large house and used to squabble over cleaning found that the best solution for them was to simply pool their money and hire a maid every two weeks. Other couples who have experienced other problems have come up with their own allocation of home task responsibilities, each as idiosyncratic as their relationship. The bottom line, Francesca has come to believe, is that there is no "one size fits all" answer to chore wars. Rather, each household must forge solutions that fit their individual strengths and weaknesses.

In her own marriage, for instance, Francesca is quick to point out that neither she nor Dirk ever wanted a perfect fifty-fifty split in either the workload or the responsibility for it. Given her nature, Francesca says it's important to her to maintain ultimate control at home—and this is an authority that Dirk does not mind ceding to her. "In the end," he says, "I think in any organization there needs to be a decision maker, and both my wife and I feel comfortable with her taking this role. But that doesn't mean we don't talk things over and jointly plan our lives."

And it doesn't mean that Dirk is simply a foot soldier carrying out the imperatives of his wife, the general. He has become more than capable of running their household by himself. There are times, for instance, when Francesca is working on a particularly difficult case, and she finds herself leaving for work before the kids wake up and returning late at night, long after they have gone to bed.

"On these occasions, I can call my husband and tell him the situation, and I know I will have complete *coverage*," she says. "I know that our kids will be taken care of by a guy who is completely capable, willing, and happy to do so."

Adds Dirk as he heads for the door to walk the dog: "She might even get a back rub when she gets home."

A Second Family's Odyssey Toward Peace

Leo Tolstoy once wrote that "Happy families are all alike; every unhappy family is unhappy in its own way." Though chore wars unhappiness certainly involves recurring themes, Tolstoy was probably right in believing that the form domestic workload strife takes is unique to every unhappy family situation. In a second family that I was able to profile in depth, the couple's therapist, Minneapolis-based Gail Hartman, agreed to give her perspective on the lengthy therapeutic process that brought them back from the brink. Indeed, when Eric and Suzanne O'Toole found their way into Hartman's office, they—like Dirk and Francesca—were giving themselves one last gasp try at saving their troubled marriage. Here is their story:

Suzanne O'Toole sometimes felt so overwhelmed by her workload that she would cry in frustration in her car on the way home at night. Her nine-to-five job creating instructional materials for companies was only the beginning of her sixteen-hour day. Like millions of other working mothers across the United States, quitting time at the corporate office only meant one thing: a race through rush hour traffic to punch the clock for the second shift at home.

Just like her mother before her, Suzanne felt a bred-in-the-bone responsibility for every aspect of her family's domestic life. Despite the demands of her full-time career, she also felt compelled to make sure the kids were thriving, the house was clean, the laundry was washed, the meals were cooked, and the books were kept.

Her husband, Eric, the forty-one-year-old owner of a tutoring business, was not completely devoid of contribution. In addition to undertaking traditional husbandly duties—mowing the lawn, car repairs, and home remodeling projects—he cooked meals occasionally and often drove the couple's three children to school.

"But I was always the one who had to *organize* the everyday chores," recalls Suzanne. "I was the one who constantly juggled the mental schedules. Eric could decide when he *wanted* to help, but, if his own schedule suddenly changed, I was just left hanging. His help was never something you could *depend* on."

Almost more than the endless chores themselves, it was this sense of unremitting responsibility—of ultimately shouldering the burden alone and without a safety net—that finally overwhelmed Suzanne. She remembers with great clarity the Memorial Day weekend three years ago when she finally snapped.

Meltdown

It was a cool, cloudless summer morning in the family's hometown of St. Paul, Minnesota. Son Billy, who was eight at the time, was outside playing. Two-year-old Faith was occupied with her building blocks on the living room floor, and the couple's eldest—eleven-year-old Julie—was doing her best to worm out of a chore Suzanne had assigned her. On the living room couch, Eric was reading the newspaper and lost in thought.

"I had already scrubbed the kitchen floor and was just finishing vacuuming the living room," recalls Suzanne, "and I thought to myself, 'Here I am again—the old Saturday morning grind.' It occurred to me that everyone else in the family was planning all of these wonderful things to do for the day, and I was just planning more chores. I suddenly found myself feeling extremely angry and used—the whole live-in maid syndrome. 'Nobody appreciates this,' I thought. 'They don't understand how much work it takes to maintain this household. How could they when they never helped do it?' So, I blew up. I just screamed, 'I have had it! This is it!' I threw down the vacuum and said, 'We are going to do something about this now.'"

Suzanne half expected her kids and husband to scramble for safety. But instead, they all rallied around, agreeing something did have to be done. In a telling disclosure three years after the fact, Eric admits he doesn't remember too many of the details of his wife's blowup, but he does recall quite clearly the atmosphere of bitterness that characterized their family life in those inequitable days.

"It was really obvious Suzanne thought the situation was unfair," says Eric. "I was very much absorbed in my business back then, and I did leave the family and household matters to Suzanne." But at the time, Eric says, he viewed his wife's relentless pursuit to complete household tasks as a compulsion of hers, one he did not buy into. Whenever she attempted to delegate chores to him, he felt nagged and bossed around. "I really felt it was the case of somebody else chewing up my time," he recalls. "I have always hated to be ordered around—it makes me dig in my heels and resist more. At this point in our marriage, Suzanne and I had reached a kind of unspoken agreement not to reach a pact for sharing."

The Letter of the Law

Fueled by Suzanne's crisis and Eric's desire to escape further criticism and blowups, the family agreed to sit down together and try to hammer out an answer to the chores problem. The solution they hit upon came from a somewhat unexpected quarter: daughter Julie, who at the time was a sixth grader in a local Montessori program.

At her school, Julie explained, the teacher had taught the children to play a chores game that worked quite well. Every individual task that needed to be done—from cleaning the blackboards to straightening up classroom shelves—was written down on a separate card. Each Monday, the teacher shuffled the cards and dealt them to the kids, who were then responsible for getting their assigned duties done that week. The O'Tooles decided it made sense to adapt the same concept to their own household duties. The first step was to list all the domestic chores.

"It was really strange and funny at first," says Julie, "because I don't think my dad really had an idea of what we did to clean the house. He had all these funny chores on the list—like *clean the toaster* or *wipe the refrigerator door.*"

With a little patient guidance from Julie and Suzanne, the family eventually whittled down the list to a realistic twenty items—including everything from shopping for groceries and folding laundry to walking the dog and cleaning the bathroom. Suzanne was hardly surprised to find that, of these twenty duties, she had regularly shouldered fifteen. "Eric sometimes cooked and the kids sometimes did a few other chores. But, only when I told them to—before the chores game, there was no buy-in for them."

But the chores game was not without logistical problems. Eight-year-old Billy, for instance, pointed out that he was not old enough to go grocery shopping and what's more, he did not know how to do many other things, such as clean the bathroom. The family worked out solutions: allowing members to swap certain chores, for instance, and to partner up on others. For the kids, especially, the game proved fun and effective—at least in the beginning. "They were empowered to be part of the family," says Suzanne. "I could see them feeling really good about it, really pleased to contribute."

But other problems were brewing. One stemmed directly from a particular chores card—the so-called Job Checker. Whichever family member was dealt this card became responsible for overseeing the quality of the rest of the family's work that week. Suzanne did not like this role—what she called the Big Mom position—because the overseer/task master identity was precisely what she was trying to escape. Daughter Julie, on the other hand, took to the role with a fervor that made her a kind of dreaded Big Mom, Jr.

"I was pretty bossy," Julie admits. "The game had been my idea and I wanted everything to go my way. I even made a little book of all the rules you had to follow to do the chores right."

Eventually Eric, who before had only had to deal with his wife bossing him around, now found himself under orders from his whole family. On the occasions when he would draw the Job Checker card himself, he typically ignored the duty entirely. Within a few weeks, he began to neglect his other assigned chores as well, or he'd wait till the last possible moment on Sunday night to finish them.

Like a man chafing under a court order, Eric found himself focusing only on the letter of the law—and complying with as little of this as he could get away with. The O'Toole children, seeing their father's behavior, soon became choristers of disapproval. "Eric still felt nagged," admits Suzanne. "Only now, it was by all of us."

"Sunday evening family meetings," Eric recalls, "became a regular opportunity to rag on Dad. That made it very difficult for me." And his heels began to dig in deeper than ever.

In time, the kids began to shirk their duties too, arguing that if Dad did not have to do his share, they should not have to do theirs either. The less work her family did, the more Suzanne found herself being inexorably sucked back into her old role: the long-suffering Big Mom. "Sometimes I'd kick myself because I'd do some of Eric's chores for him." And then Julie's. And Billy's.

Within several months, a "solution" that had seemed so promising had simply circled Suzanne and Eric back to their original roles. The only change was Suzanne felt more hopeless than ever. Eventually, she and Eric felt so stuck they decided to seek help from a third party.

The Spirit of the Law

When psychologist Gail Hartman, forty-four, first saw the O'Tooles for marriage counseling, she perceived in their troubles a very familiar story: two decent people who obviously loved each other, but who had somehow become fixed in patterns that were causing them both great unhappiness.

"I felt *empathy* with Suzanne and *sympathy* for Eric," recalls Hartman. "I felt this connection to Suzanne because I could sense as a woman where she was coming from. And I liked Eric instantly. By this point, he was so tortured by this problem that I found him very endearing."

In Hartman's view, Suzanne's hopelessness was quite understandable. In addition to a full-time job outside the home, Suzanne's role in the family was nothing short of a hyperstressed air traffic controller. "Suzanne was very overworked," says Hartman. "And she felt hopeless at ever being able to convince her husband to do anything different than what he was already doing."

In Eric, on the other hand, Hartman saw a man who was deeply preoccupied by his own business concerns, a man who also felt lonely and beset upon by his wife and kids. "He felt like a nagged, failed partner," says Hartman. "He'd sometimes make promises like, 'I will clean the toilet.' And then he would not do it, so that even his kids stopped believing his word. I think he felt guilty, but that was not how he presented himself."

Instead, says Hartman, Eric maintained that he was doing the best he could—that the *real* problem, at least in part, was that his wife was constantly overmanaging the household.

But the more Hartman got to know the O'Tooles, however, the more she realized such a scenario just did not apply to their family life.

Suzanne's housecleaning standards were hardly extreme—she simply needed some help in managing the household and family she and her husband had created together. Hartman sensed that the couple's root problem was deeper than a simple matter of reallocating chores. "Eric felt like a failure—he did not know how to bring pleasure to his wife," says Hartman. "Holding on to his stance was almost like cutting off his nose to spite his face." Admits Suzanne today: "I really think my husband had come to believe that making me happy was almost impossible."

Fights over housework, Hartman had learned from counseling many couples in trouble, are not a simple matter of who sweeps the floor or cleans the toilet. Such fights have roots to a host of profound, core issues, from intimacy and sharing responsibility to balance of power and each person's sense of self-worth.

"There is an expression I like a lot," says Eric today. " 'Change is inevitable, but growth is optional.' " Over the course of what would prove to be twenty-two counseling sessions with Hartman spread out over the next year, both Eric and Suzanne acknowledge today that their relationship not only changed, it grew—tremendously.

"It feels just *wonderful*," says Suzanne. "It's like a great weight has been lifted off my shoulders. Once we got our relationship in order, the housework just slipped into place. Those awful fights about who does what have just stopped."

"It's really been hugely significant," agrees Eric. "It feels great. The vocabulary seems so limited when trying to describe it. Such a profound change has taken place in our relationship."

That the O'Tooles were able to so successfully move from point A to point B says a lot about their commitment to each other and their willingness to negotiate entrenched behaviors that had become almost perversely comfortable in their familiarity. But as clear-cut as their progress now seems in retrospect, both agree that for every two steps forward, they often took one backward—a situation very reminiscent of Dirk and Francesca's progress toward harmony. Still, with the help of Hartman, the O'Tooles did reach a real solution to a problem that had theretofore eluded their own best attempts to solve. Some of the milestones in their therapy included:

Understanding the Context in Which the Problem Grew

One of the first questions Hartman had for Suzanne and Eric was about their own families of origin. Suzanne had grown up one of eleven children in a farm family. She and her sisters were expected to help their mother with household chores as well as help their brothers do work outside. "My brothers never helped clean the house," says Suzanne, "even though we girls were expected to be outside helping with the animals. Even as I was growing up, I thought, 'This is really nuts. I will never have this kind of system.'"

Eric, for his part, grew up the oldest of five children. "There was a clear distinction in our house regarding Mom's work and Dad's work," he recalls, though this distinction did not apply to the children. "For us kids, it was expected we do any and all housework we were asked to do." Eric cooked, which he liked, but he also ironed and did "a lot of dishes"—tasks that he hated and that his father never had to do. Eric recalls clearly how his mother constantly nagged him to do chores—and how much he hated being nagged.

Suzanne and Eric both came of age in the sixties, a time when gender stereotypes were undergoing critical reevaluation. "In a way," says Hartman, "they had a fairly evolved relationship. They knew the roles they had grown up with were not exactly the ones they wanted to live out in their marriage."

But once again intellectual understanding proved to be a lot different than emotional acceptance. The O'Tooles, like many other couples of their era, found it easier to slip back into the parental roles they had had modeled for them as kids. For Suzanne, this meant becoming a Big Mom; for Eric, it meant remaining the Big Kid—and stubbornly resisting all efforts to boss him around the house.

Defining a Vision for How Things Could Be Better

It did not take long for Suzanne and Eric to both acknowledge that they truly did want to escape these roles and forge a different kind of relationship. Hartman encouraged them to begin by really empathizing with the other's position. Eric came to realize that his wife's chronic overload at home was not just an excuse to be bossy, but, rather, an issue that deeply hurt her. Suzanne, for her part, came to understand that her husband's behavior was less a matter of laziness than a reflection of how truly powerless he was feeling at home.

As adversarial as they had become in recent years, there had been occasions in their marriage when the two had pulled together. Once, for instance, during a week at a rural camp, the entire O'Toole family had experienced how rewarding it can be when everyone has to work together for the common good. Eric, especially, was inspired by the all-for-one generosity everyone showed.

Says Suzanne today, "It's really critical to envision how you would like things to be. It was a lot more comfortable for me to sit there and whine about what I did not like." But once she and Eric were able to articulate a shared vision of what they *did* want, they were able to begin taking steps to get there.

Seeing the Value of Helping Your Mate

One of the first suggestions Hartman made to Eric was that he could gain a sense of power and joy in his relationship by learning to take care of—and bring pleasure to—his wife. For both Eric and Suzanne, who prided themselves on a certain independent spirit, this notion of positive caretaking required a major shift in thinking.

"I did not look at 'taking care' of other people as a healthy thing to do," admits Eric. "To me it seemed like co-dependency—you just go around sticking your nose into other people's lives, even if they don't need it. I viewed Suzanne as a very strong woman who was not really in need of me. The idea of taking care of her was a very strange notion."

"Gail talked a lot about us taking care of each other," says Suzanne. "She used the term *sacredness* in describing it. I remember long into therapy, Gail asked Eric, 'How can you take care of Suzanne?' He said, 'I don't know.' I started to try and give some suggestions, and Gail said to wait—that he needed to think of some ideas on his own."

Hartman's specific challenge to the couple: Come back next week and tell me some of the ways you found to take care of each other. Slowly, by hit and miss, the two began to find opportunities to help each other. Eric started escorting his wife on nightly walks in their neighborhood—something she greatly enjoyed but had been reluctant to do by herself after dark. Another example occurred when Eric cleaned the bathroom. He noticed the mirror was dirty and actually shined it up on his own initiative.

In therapy the next week, Eric was astonished to find how much this small gesture meant to his wife. "You mean, that's it?" he said to Hartman. "That's all it takes?"

"Suzanne," said Hartman, "can you tell Eric why that gave you hope?"

"I didn't have to prod you," Suzanne replied to her husband. "It made me realize you were aware—that you looked, you cared, you did it knowing that now someone else in the family would not have to. You're beginning to catch on."

What Eric was catching onto was a sea change in attitude. Rather than viewing housework solely as something he had to do for Suzanne, he was slowly but surely learning to view it as a responsibility he himself owned—a responsibility akin to others he had long held, such as providing for his family financially and making sure his children received a top-notch education.

Over a period of months, Eric was strongly encouraged in his changes by positive feedback from both his wife and Hartman. He also noticed that the more space Suzanne gave him to take responsibility at home, the more willing he was to do it.

"Maybe," he told Suzanne during one session, "part of why I am doing more around the house is that you are not bugging me about it so much."

"That *is* part of the solution, isn't it?" Hartman asked Suzanne.

Learning to Let Go

As much as Suzanne felt burdened by her Big Mom role, it was not easy for her to surrender control. For one thing, she was still not convinced Eric would always come through and pick up the slack she gave him. All too easily, she could envision what she calls "every woman's nightmare"—friends dropping over unexpectedly only to find a messy, chaotic household that reflected negatively on Suzanne's self-worth.

Partly, Suzanne admits today, surrendering authority at home meant losing part of her self. "I did not want to be responsible for the entire household," she says. "But this also meant I had to give up power. It was, in a way, really scary for me. This was part of my identity in the family."

Suzanne also realized that she would have to alter her domestic standards—not necessarily lower them, but acknowledge that for Eric and the kids to truly share responsibility, she would have to allow him to work in his own way and on his own timetable.

It's unrealistic to expect your spouse to be exactly like yourself, Hartman explained. And women who hold such a standard are practically guaranteeing disappointment for themselves. Recalls Hartman: "As Eric was starting to make his own changes, he would say, 'I can promise to do the bathroom this week, but I can't promise to do it before noon.' Suzanne had to learn to tolerate his timeline. This was absolutely reasonable and necessary, but it was hard for her."

One way Hartman helped Suzanne loosen the reins was to encourage her to find other activities to fill up the time she formerly spent controlling all aspects of the household. "A lot of energy goes into nagging," says Hartman. "Suzanne needed to find some other things to do with all that energy—such as spending more time with her friends or pursuing projects from work."

One example of how Suzanne eventually changed was her reevaluation of Saturday chores. "It was almost habitual with me—I felt Saturday chores had to be done on Saturday mornings," she says. "Eric didn't believe that that was the case. I had to look at it and ask myself why it was so important to me. I realized it was just something I had always done that way. And I learned I could let it pass. My alternative was to take back the role of Big Mom, and say, 'Do it now,' but I knew I didn't want that. It felt so much better to have Eric contributing."

The Upward Spiral

Like dancers learning a new step, Eric and Suzanne slowly came into harmony with each other. The more responsibility that Eric accepted, the less stressed-out Suzanne felt, and the less need she felt to compel his domestic work. The more space Suzanne gave her husband to act, the more rewarding Eric found it to be a full contributing partner at home.

"All of a sudden," says Hartman, "the problem was spiraling upward instead of downward. He did more, she felt better, and her patience was reinforced by the fact that he followed through on a lot of his promises. This, in turn, made her give him great feedback. I remember during one session, Suzanne said to her husband, 'You know, this feels like it is working,' and he answered, 'Yes—it's starting to feel a lot better.'"

Three years later, the new roles the O'Tooles learned during therapy continue to invigorate their marriage and family life with a sense of mutuality and partnership. Today, the whole family still plays the chores game adapted from Julie's classroom—but there are two main differences from their first experience with it.

For one thing, everyone now views the game only as a tool, not a prescription, for getting jobs done. The second change is that the card for Job Checker has been thrown away.

"We took that job out, all right," says Suzanne. "We realized we didn't need it anymore."

Perhaps the greatest beneficiaries of the parental changes are the O'Toole kids themselves. Billy, for instance, says that when he gets married someday, he plans on emulating his parents' approach to shared responsibility.

Eldest daughter Julie, who in earlier generations would have almost certainly been groomed to become a Big Mom herself, says she has learned a better way to interact with her own future husband and children. "I definitely benefitted from seeing my parents work things out," sums up Julie. "Not everyone is going to be exactly like you, and I have learned that to solve problems, you have to work together."

Checklist

To be sure, condensing the lessons of therapy into an enumerated checklist is a bit like summarizing how to play the game of golf in a pamphlet. In both cases, a quick-take synopsis can be useful, but only up to a point. If your own chore wars are relatively minor, keeping the following steps in mind may help you foster open communication and remain on an even keel.

But if your problems are causing serious distress in your relationship, you may find that understanding these steps intellectually does not translate into living them emotionally. In such cases, you might want to seek the help of a counselor as a kind of objective "change coach," trained to help you both learn new and better ways to interact as a team. (More on this at the end of the next chapter.)

For now, here are a few therapeutic milestones to consider on your own path to peace:

- Determine if you have a problem. Even if your household has run smoothly for years, big family changes—from the advent of children to a new job for a previously stay-at-home partner—can really alter the household dynamics, rendering once workable patterns obsolete.

- Don't assume your partner knows what you're feeling. Is one of you consistently overburdened on the homefront? If so, don't keep your feelings bottled inside in the hopes your partner will read your mood *and* your mind. Set aside a regular time to talk over how your household is running—and what contributions each of you would like the other to make so that your home life *feels* fairer to everyone who lives there.

- Honestly try to empathize with your partner, to see things from his or her perspective. Again, don't assume you know what the other is thinking and feeling. Ask!

- Consider the housework roles you each grew up with and discuss whether these roles still make sense in your household. If you're committed to living in a different kind of relationship than your parents did, realize that you will sometimes need to consciously overcome the emotional momentum of your upbringing.

- Be honest with *yourself* about your own feelings. What jobs, for instance, do you really want the other person to assume, and which ones do you want to keep control over? For many women, especially, ambivalence about domestic roles is a fact of life. But if you're feeling this way and *don't* acknowledge it, you risk sending mixed messages that can leave your partner utterly baffled about what changes to make.

- Realize that there is a big difference between doing a chore when asked versus taking responsibility for it. If your partner doesn't understand how to own a household task, discuss with him other areas of life where he has traditionally taken responsibility—and help him transfer those feelings to the domestic domain.

- Understand that change will not be sustainable without compromise. If it's true that one partner needs to learn to take greater responsibility and shoulder more work at home, it's probably also true that the other partner must surrender some control and provide her with room to operate. By the same token, standards of performance cannot be decided 100 percent by one partner. Compromise is key.

- Realize that a detailed chore schedule spelling out everything that needs to be done, by whom, how well, and on what timetable is not likely to be the ultimate solution to chore wars. Until each household member understands and embraces "the spirit of the law," all attempts to mandate "the letter of the law" will only result in a furious search for loopholes. In this sense, a Big Boss' decrees share much in common with the U.S. Tax Code.

- Remember that household work, despite its history of low-paid status, is nevertheless skilled work. It takes time for rookies to learn and master necessary skills—a process that will occur much more quickly when progress is encouraged with rewards and praise, not punishments and criticism.

- Try to set aside a regular time for fun. Between your jobs and your domestic duties, life can sometimes seem like an infinite "to do" list, with two new items springing up for every one you manage to cross off. Get a baby-sitter if you need one, and enjoy a date at least once a week so the two of you can relax, have fun, and reconnect.

- Ultimately, try to see sharing at home as an expression of love that truly builds upon itself. The happier and less stressed one partner becomes, the better off his or her mate will likewise be. This is true for children in the household, as well. Not only will youngsters benefit from the general atmosphere of domestic peace, they'll also learn from firsthand experience roles that will help ensure harmony in their own future relationships.

Chapter 5

CHORES AND PEACE

Practical Strategies to End the War

*It is common sense to take a method and try it. If it fails,
admit it frankly and try another. But above all, try something.*
—Franklin D. Roosevelt

Never go to bed angry. Stay up and fight.
—Phyllis Diller

Advice is least heeded when most needed.
—English proverb

*A wrong-doer is often a man that has left something undone,
not always he who has done something.*
—Marcus Aurelius

*Patience is power; with time and patience the mulberry leaf
becomes silk.*
—Chinese proverb

Lynette's Story

"Robert and I have been married three and a half years now, and we are fairly compatible with chore division, except when company is expected. Then I, hearing the rather insistent voice of my raised-by-Germans-and-nuns mother, go into a full-bore cleaning frenzy. On these occasions—dinner parties, other parties, but especially the overnight visits of relatives—I go nuts and try to clean everything; dusting, vacuuming, mopping, and tidying up a storm. Don't forget the fresh flowers in every room.

"Rob, on the other hand, seems to feel no such compulsion. I suppose that women still feel judged by the cleanliness of their houses, despite feminism. I typically only resent this when it is his family I am cleaning for.

"Otherwise, we split things pretty fairly, possibly because each of us lived alone for many years and were thus used to taking care of ourselves. This fairness and harmony is admittedly helped along by the relative ease of our lifestyle: Rob works at home, I work at the university, we live in a 1,200 square foot house, and we have no children or pets.

"Fortunately for the sake of harmony, we are both naturally neat people. Unfortunately for the sake of our home's overall sanitation, neither of us is excessively clean. Result: Little apparent clutter but plenty of outsized dust bunnies. Indeed the dust bunny population reached such a size last winter that during a mice invasion I once mistook a largish dust bunny for a smallish mouse and in a fit of hysterics called Rob in Wisconsin about said supposed mouse, though God knows what he could have done about it from 250 miles away.

"My best advice for marital chore harmony is to marry someone similar to you on the neat/clean axis, or, failing that, to pay someone else to clean up occasionally. This stuff is really not worth fighting about."

Robert's Story

"Lynette and I blessedly are of the same basic human type: neat but not overly clean. Which means we're overall quite content with each other and don't get on each other's nerves . . . too much.

"But let's step back to our first impressions when we met. She was horrified by the state of my bathroom (filthy), and I was horrified by the state of her kitchen (crusty). This pattern continues. She routinely cleans the bathroom because I'm not horrified by a stray whisker in the sink; I probably spend more time wiping grease off the stove, scraping pesto off the refrigerator, excavating sesame seeds from the cutting board, and scrubbing newspaper ink off the counter than she does, simply because I don't want to eat in that environment.

"We also have another traditional split in that I have zero tolerance for cooking or thinking about food but don't mind cleaning up. So Lynette does 99 percent of the cooking, and I most often clean up. Of course, this causes a certain amount of stress. She's an extremely messy cook (why use two pans when you can use five?), and I get a bit testy about cleaning up so much (I feel) unnecessary mess.

"I don't mind grocery shopping, but if she cooks, she has to make a list, and her list and my assumptions never jibe. This can be a good source of stress and tension—would you, for instance, naturally assume the listed item "tomatoes" means three sixteen-ounce cans of Hunt's stewed tomatoes? We've compromised now and generally shop together, which is fun.

"Another unique aspect of our housekeeping division: We both do our own laundry. This is the result of living on our own for too long before getting married. I previously lived with a woman and we tried sharing laundry, but once upon a time I opened the dryer and leaped back in horror. It looked like fresh road kill, like a beaver had been sucked in one end of a turbocharger and spit out the other end in the dryer.

"Turns out Marcia had left a tube of lipstick in her pocket. I purge all pockets before throwing clothes in the hamper; she went through pockets before throwing clothes in the washer itself. Anyway, the clothes were a total loss, she was mad at me, I was mad at her, and to this day I do my own laundry. (And who says men can't learn?)

"Another source of conflict is in our upbringing. Lynette's mother maintained her household with military spit and polish. Major housecleaning every Saturday. Lynette didn't inherit her mother's standard, but did inherit tremendous guilt and a vision of how things ought to be, which surfaces whenever we have company. She'll fly into a major cleaning snit because, *What will the company think?*

"My mother, on the other hand, was an indifferent housekeeper at best, so if the house is a little dusty, who cares? Guests aren't coming to white-glove our bookshelves, are they? My policy is to keep the lights low and build a fire to distract them from noticing the dust bunnies.

"When I do clean, however, I get totally obsessed and rush about the house in a state of maniacal possession, practically foaming at the mouth for two or three hours. This scares Lynette almost as much as my not cleaning irritates her. Man cannot win.

"Men, I do think, feel more judged by the state of their car, even if, like myself, they're not particularly into cars. When we met, Lynette used the back of her car as a portable trash can, and she will still happily pitch a newspaper or candy wrapper over her shoulder into the back seat, and if I didn't clean the car it would sit there for months. I'm much more particular about the car, keeping it neat and clean . . . even as it rusts."

Self-Help Strategies

As Lynette and Robert's good-natured repartee indicates, the chore wars don't have to be, well, wars at all. Call them chore sores, maybe, vexatious little bumps that only occasionally get noticed at all—and then are more a source of embarrassment than pain.

If you and your mate generally have no problem communicating and yet you're still afflicted by the benign minisquabbles of Lynette and Robert, psychologists suggest that there are a range of different strategies you might want to try on your own.

For the past fourteen years, Michele Weiner-Davis, M.S.W., author of *Divorce Busting,* has practiced a model of solution-oriented, brief therapy that generally lasts no more than four to six sessions. Her approach rejects several conventions of traditional psychotherapy in favor of "whatever works" pragmatism. Call it domestic *realpolitik.*

For one thing, says Weiner-Davis, a couple's past is usually irrelevant. "Looking at a couple's social history and backgrounds," she explains, "is an introspective journey that leads, in my opinion, nowhere. You can have all the insight in the world about how you got stuck, but still not have a clue as to how to get unstuck."

Weiner-Davis recommends that the person in the relationship more irritated by the situation take steps to initiate change—and not hold his or her breath waiting for the other person to act first. "It's not always the woman who is more bothered, but ninety-five times out of a hundred it is," she explains. "Since women are more often defining the situation as a problem, I believe they have to take responsibility for figuring out a way to resolve it. This may not be politically correct, but it is more efficient. True equality may be the ideal. But if you've tried talking it out and realize that it's not going to happen, I think the wife needs to focus on what is changeable rather than locking horns and being miserable."

For those interested in trying Weiner-Davis's pragmatic approach at home, here's what she suggests. It works equally well with spouses, children, or recalcitrant roommates.

Realize It Only Takes One to Tango

If you really want the situation to change, don't sit around waiting for the other person to change first. Altering your own behavior in a significant way is like tipping over the first domino—the other person's changes will inevitably follow.

Try Backing Off

It's almost a rule of nature: The more work one person does, the less the other does. Don't say anything—just stop doing a few chores and wait and see what happens. But be prepared to wait a long time—probably longer than you would like to.

Actions Speak Louder Than Words

Women tend to communicate their requests verbally—that is, if you want your partner to do something, you ask him to do it. If this fails, odds are you'll just ask again—but in a louder and angrier voice. This tends to make him feel you're trying to control him, and he becomes even *less* likely to do what you want. So instead of talking, try taking creative action. One example: For fifty years, one wife had pleaded with her husband not to come to the dinner table with his shirt off. For fifty years, he had ignored her requests. But after reading Weiner-Davis' advice, she decided to try taking off her own shirt at the dinner table. Her husband never ate shirtless again.

Be Specific by Breaking Down Your Requests for Help into Concrete Behaviors

Instead of asking the other person to be more helpful, ask him, for example, to drive the kids to school twice a week and be in charge of washing the dishes nightly.

Praise Don't Criticize

Whenever he or she does help out, even if it's only on a hit-or-miss basis, reward the hits and be less critical of the misses. This point can't be overemphasized—it's frustrating for anybody to feel they can't do something right, and too much of this frustration leads to avoiding the task altogether.

Pick Your Battles

Many people not only want their spouses or kids to help at home, they want them to want to help. This may be the ideal, but it's often not realistic. Rather than concentrating on a whole-scale personality makeover, pick several specific behaviors the other person could work on to help you.

If the Other Person Needs Reminding, Remind Him or Her

Many children, housemates, or spouses will gladly help if asked. More chore aware people can make themselves miserable about the fact that their family members don't volunteer to help—or they can focus instead on the fact that a little gentle reminding often gets the job done.

Try Applying the Golden Rule

When one wife complained that her husband no longer treated her nicely, Weiner-Davis suggested as an experiment that she go out of her way to be nice to him. The wife started packing her husband's lunch each morning, including a short love note. Very soon afterward, her husband's whole attitude changed. Not only did he begin treating his wife more nicely, but he pitched in more around the house.

If All Else Fails, Buy a Solution

Weiner-Davis acknowledges that hiring a housekeeper is not an option for everyone, but even those who can afford it don't always "give themselves permission" to obtain outside help. "This may sound like a cop-out, but I've worked with so many couples where it's made a big difference in their lives. They wonder why they waited so long."

From Adversaries to Teammates

Helpful as Weiner-Davis' approach can be for many households, sometimes the problem is so deeply entrenched that behavioral change alone is not enough. In families like the O'Tooles, for instance, where the chore wars tensions had a long, deep-seated history, the only chance for reaching a lasting accord depended on the combatants making profound attitudinal changes in their relationship. Time and again, psychologists echoed the essential nature of this reconfiguration: Stop viewing your partner as an adversary and learn to cooperate with him or her as a teammate. This sounds simple and self-evident in theory—but, in reality, it can be fiendishly difficult to get some households to even give it a try. Imagine a group hug between trucking industry executives and the Teamster's Union, and you begin to glimpse how alien a concept cooperation can be in many families. Still, the shift from adversaries to helpmates is not only possible, but, once it comes, it can seem simple in retrospect.

"Couples can definitely change—I see it happening all the time," says therapist Marcia Lasswell, M.A., the president of the American

Association for Marriage and Family Therapy. "And life is so easy once you learn to cooperate."

It Takes Two

In some relationships, one or both partners can harbor deep-rooted impediments to a teamwork approach. Sometimes, says Lasswell, a spouse feels he or she *needs* to win to avoid feeling weak or devalued. Indeed, some men and women believe that if they don't hold their ground, they'll be swallowed up by the other. If your partner occasionally comes off like a tyrant or bully, odds are it's *not* because they perceive themselves as strong. "Tyranny," says Lasswell, "almost always stems from insecurity."

In the most deep-seated cases, such feelings may need to be untangled in therapy. But there *are* things you can try on your own before taking this step. First, think about the activities you and your partner have done cooperatively in the past. Perhaps you have cooked a complicated meal together or worked on a home improvement project where it took four hands to get the job done. With couples who have trouble thinking of *anything* they've cooperated on, Lasswell often gives out a fun but illuminating assignment: Rent a tandem bicycle and go for a long ride together in the countryside. Another exercise that really mandates cooperation is hanging wallpaper—a project that is virtually impossible for one person to do alone.

Once you have experienced several such cooperative situations, discuss how it felt to approach a common goal as a team instead of as two individuals. Did one person always lead and the other follow, or did you find yourself incorporating good ideas from both parties? Ask yourselves how it felt to achieve success together—rather than one of you winning and the other losing. The point of both doing and discussing these cooperative ventures is that you will both begin to build a team mindset that can generalize throughout the far reaches of your relationship. The more success you have winning together, the less likely either will feel they are being taken advantage of or somehow losing out to the other.

Make It Their Problem, Too

Women often bear the brunt of chore wars suffering, in part, because women are so much more likely to be judged negatively if basic standards are not upheld. Say your son or daughter goes to school in obviously dirty clothing—who do you think will be held responsible, the father or the mother?

Many men, Lasswell says, were brought up to believe that their time truly is better spent on making a living than doing housework. Modern women, on the other hand, have received mixed messages—excel in a career, sure, but also stay the course your stay-at-home mother set for the household.

Because of these larger forces, the chore wars are practically guaranteed to leave many women in a quandary and many men relatively clueless about what's wrong. But rather than waiting till gross inequity at home brings you to a boiling point, Lasswell suggests women broach the subject with their partner during a calm period. "The overworked spouse *has* to let the other one know she's unhappy," says Lasswell. "She might try saying something like this: 'I don't like how this is going—I don't think it's fair. And I think we need to do something about it, because I am finding that I'm angry with you a lot, and that I am not very sexually responsive. I think the problem is going to get worse, and I don't think you want that.'

"By approaching the problem this way," says Lasswell, "what the woman is doing, in essence, is making it *his* problem, too. He may not think that housework is a problem, but he sure may think her withdrawal and anger and cutting off sex is a problem."

If, after such a discussion, the man still truly doesn't care, the woman needs to examine the relationship to see if she wants it to continue. Most of the time, fortunately, men can be surprisingly accommodating. "Men respond very positively to the word *fair*," says Lasswell. "They are very logical about it, and, if they feel they have a say in setting the standards, men can definitely change and work toward mutual goals with their wives."

Children and teens, too, will usually respond well to a heartfelt request for fairness—provided the requester approaches the subject calmly and in a spirit of cooperative problem-solving. What isn't likely to work with kids and spouses alike is an angry mandate: Do this the way I say, when I say, or else! Remember: Winning teams may have a leader, but they rarely win with a dictator at the helm.

Defining the Job

With the O'Toole family, we saw how one of the first steps in changing chores behavior depends upon understanding and taking to heart "the spirit of the law." But at some point, it also becomes necessary to attend to "the letter of the law" as well.

In a way, running a household is not unlike running a successful business. If you don't have a cooperative mission to focus your goals and energies, chances are you'll flounder and founder. But a mission in and of itself is not enough—you also need to pay attention to the details of the day-to-day operations. In a household, like a factory, this means first taking stock of what exactly needs to be done.

Chances are the woman in a relationship already knows, in her bones, the intricacies of what needs to be done. Chances are that the man and children, on the other hand, only know that there's "pretty much, probably."

Consider how the mates in one revealing relationship view their mutual household workload.

Tim's Story

"I came from a relatively large family of five children. In part due to the size of our household, there were more chores to do, and more people to do them, so there was always just an expectation that we kids would undertake a big share of the housework. And because all five of us kids were relatively close age-wise, there was also a lot of sibling pressure to do this work. I mean it was physical pressure. You do it or you got knocked around by your big brother.

"We had a little chart posted on the refrigerator that specified on a rotating basis which of us had to wash the dishes on any given night, which one dried the dishes, and which one swept the floor. We each had to thoroughly clean our rooms once a week, and on Saturdays we had yard work and other chores mandated by our father. He'd come home from work at noon on Saturdays and say, 'I need some help cleaning out the garage.' Or he'd have us meet him at his office, and we'd clean up there for him.

"My dad's a judge now, though he was a small town lawyer when we were growing up. I suppose you could say raising us helped prepare him for the judiciary—he got a lot of practice meting out justice on his children.

"There were no household skills that I didn't learn how to do over the course of my childhood. I know how to sweep a floor, for instance, and I've been known to grab the broom from the hands of a person who I don't feel is sweeping properly. Basically, I don't like to clean, and, when I do it, I like to do it with alacrity. When I see someone dilly-dallying over a broom, my tendency is to say, 'Gimme that,' and sweep it quickly.

"My wife, Susan, came from a much different background. Her parents divorced when she was young, and her mother was not always around. She and her sister basically undertook a lot of the household duties on their own. They were fixing dinner for themselves, for instance, when they were eleven and twelve years old.

"To this day, Susan is more likely than me to *initiate* chores at home. I, on the other hand, remain a quick *finisher*—think of a twelve-year-old boy on a Saturday afternoon having to do chores with his father and wanting to go out and play baseball or football instead. You get a sense of how I approached chores then, and how I approach chores now. I want to get them over with.

"Susan and her sister, on the other hand, did not have a systematic approach to chores—it was more like they did it on instinct, undertaking different jobs whenever they felt it was appropriate to do so. I think these differences continue today in the household Susan and I have created for our own family. Susan will just wake up one morning with a feeling that something needs to be done—say, cleaning the back of the refrigerator. I prefer to have things spelled out and scheduled in advance—that way, I know what I'm going to have to do and when, and I can plan my free time accordingly."

Susan's Story

"It is hard to describe exactly how I know when it's time to clean our house. It's not like I wait until we can write our names in the dust on the floor, which I sometimes think is what Tim would like. I want the house to smell and feel clean—I don't like it when there's a grittiness when I walk barefoot on the floor. I'll wake up and all of a sudden the house is too dirty—the carpets are too dirty even to walk on, and the bathrooms are just grimy.

"Tim says I'll prod him to help, prod being somewhere between a reminder and a nag. In my view, I start out with a polite request for his help. But then if he doesn't cooperate, it does become a nag. This doesn't happen very often, though, because we really do a pretty good job of alternating almost all the household chores, from cooking to laundry. The one exception is serious housecleaning.

"It's not that Tim doesn't ever initiate projects. I'll tell you a story about this that drove me absolutely crazy. This summer, he decided on a whim to just clean all of our windows. We have a *lot* of windows. While our six-month-old twins were napping, he got out the ladders and started this huge project, which in my opinion was way too much work for what it was worth. What bugged me was how completely spontaneous a thing this was. I ended up helping him because it was far too much work for him to do all by himself.

"Tim thinks his initiating the window cleaning is the same thing I do when I wake up and decide it's time to clean the house. It's not, because cleaning is not a *monumental* task. To clean our house to the standards I would like takes basically an hour of time if we work together. But cleaning all of our windows is an all-day job. It's something we should have *planned* to do.

"Now that we have the twins, I think we are both leaning toward a more systematic schedule for the household chores. We both work full-time, and there's only so much time left over. Some days, we can keep up with the dishes and the laundry, and that's about it.

"I'm coming around to the idea that a schedule would make keeping up with the work a more orderly, predictable process. That's assuming, of course, we can find the time to do the chores we write down.

Sometimes it can be hard even finding enough time to get to the gas station to change the oil."

A Master List and the Art of Compromise

As is the case with Tim and Susan, men and women often require different signals to get them started. For some women, it's almost as if they have an inner Chores Dayrunner that alerts them, without the need for conscious thought, when a job needs to be done. For such women, it is intuitively obvious that the floors need to be washed and the back of the refrigerator denuded of gunk. Not only does this inner Chores Dayrunner ring a cerebral bell whenever it's time to do a job—it also sends a jolt of juice to the brain's worry lobe, a jolt that says, *You've got to do this now! The filth!*

There's a good side and bad side to being piloted by instinct. The good side is that the complex and multiple jobs of the household are efficiently controlled and regulated without having to squander much conscious thought on them. The bad side comes from assuming that everyone processes household information in this way, that the husband's or children's monumental lack of awareness *has* to be some kind of passive-aggressive act.

Many of us guys just process information in a different way—discrete jobs that can further be broken down into discrete steps handled one at a time in what is perceived to be rational order. It helps to write assignments down—an external Chores Dayrunner, if you will, that spells out precisely what to do when, where, and how.

Women, of course, find such dependence on a set of codified instructions a nonsensical waste of time. *Just notice,* they say. *Do things when they need to be done!* Sometimes they add an even more hellish coup de grace: *If you loved me, you'd notice!*

When men and children listen to such sentiments, what they really hear is this: Chores are a bewildering, Kafkaesque series of imperatives that can, without warning, strike at any time, making it impossible to ever have any fun. If she loved me, she wouldn't constantly make me do things out of the blue!

The bottom line is that families must work together, tapping into their strengths, to come up with a plan of action that works. Since chances are good that the woman is already doing more than her fair share, chances are also good that a plan of action will depend, in part, on codified lists and schedules that will help others initiate action despite their lack of an internal motivator.

Until I sat down and started making a list of my own family's chores, I truly had no idea how multitudinous they were. Not only did the sheer numbers give me a new respect for my wife's contributions, but creating a one-stop inventory helped me to see ways that I—and later my children—could better share a role, and how we might plan together to do things more efficiently.

A Different Kind of Twelve-Step Program

The AAMFT's Marcia Lasswell recommends a step-by-step method to help households logically divide all the chores that they *agree* need to be done, from making beds to food shopping. Here is her approach:

Step 1. Each partner should independently jot down all the household tasks that he or she feels absolutely must be done. (For a little help in getting started, you can refer to Jim Sexton's list at the end of Chapter 2. Just remember, though Sexton's list may be exhausting, it's by no means *exhaustive*. Where, for instance, is the huge job of planning and orchestrating holiday entertainment, or the nausea-inducing task of filing this year's bewildering array of IRS documents?)

Step 2. Once you have each compiled your list, exchange it with your partner's. Such comparisons can be illuminating—just seeing all the various tasks that go into household management enumerated in one place will give both spouses a sense of respect for the breadth of the work involved—and heightened appreciation for the one who has been doing most of it. But beware, less domestically involved spouse: Sometimes this exercise can prove embarrassing. In one couple who tried this exercise, the wife easily came up with dozens of tasks, whereas her husband could think only of six, one of which was patting the dog.

Amusing as such an imbalance can be, remember that you're both on the same side—*this isn't a competition over whose list is longer!* Survey your mate's inventory of chores and add anything that you forgot but that you agree needs to be done.

Step 3. Once you have both made your own lists, sit down together and compile a master list containing everything you both can agree needs to be done. If there are items that one of you considers necessary and the other considers optional, like redecorating a room, don't debate the point now—simply place such items on a supplemental list and set it aside for now. Note: If you have children, they can take part in this list-making process, too. The more each member of the household feels that he or she has had significant input, the more they will feel like contributing members of the household.

Step 4. Now that you have the master list, go through it item by item, discussing the frequency and standards of performance that you can both agree are reasonable. For instance, both people may agree that the kitchen floor needs to be mopped periodically—but one person thinks once a month is plenty, whereas the other would like to see it mopped every night after supper. "You're both going to have to compromise," says Lasswell. "Men can be convinced to do more, but only if they feel they have a reasonable say-so in the standards. I think women are going to have to work very hard to lower their standards—and let men do the job their way. In the end, the job is not going to be done exactly the way she wants it, and it's not going to be just like he wants it either. It will be somewhere in the middle."

As far as very young kids are concerned, the parents will probably need to set the standards of acceptable performance for them. But as your youngsters grow into teenagers, they should be allowed to have an increasing degree of input on the process. The more you treat them as responsible adults, the more they are likely to behave that way.

Step 5. Remember to approach the art of compromise in good faith. This is *not* litigation—it's much closer to mediation. A common negotiation technique, for instance, is to shoot for the stars so that the ultimate compromise is actually where you really hoped to end up in the first place. Example: She says the kitchen floor needs to be mopped every fifteen minutes; he says once every Olympiad is more than enough. If you find yourself sounding a bit like one of Donald Trump's lawyers, you're on the wrong track. Stop, take a deep breath, and really work at coming up with a compromise that leaves you feeling okay.

Also, if you find yourselves disagreeing about how a job should be done, be willing to discuss why you feel a certain way—and be honest about it. In one couple, Hillary agreed to do the laundry, which included folding the washed clothing before putting it away. She actually enjoyed this latter task, which she would do while watching TV in the family room. Kara, however, took exception to this. She instructed Hillary to take the clean clothes upstairs and fold them on the bed. When asked *why* she insisted he do it this way, Kara eventually had to admit the only reason was that that was how she always had always done it. "And that," says Lasswell, "is not a reasonable reason."

Work your way through the master list *quickly*. If you reach an impasse at any point, simply move the item over to the supplemental list to be handled later. Your goal now is to agree on as much as possible as quickly as you can.

Step 6. Now that your Master List spells out not only what you agree should be done, but also how you agree it should be acceptably done, it's time to start divvying things up. Lasswell advises her clients to each take a copy of the list to separate quarters and independently rate each item on a score from one to four. "One" is a chore you most *want* to do. "Two" is a chore that you will do, though you don't necessarily want to do. "Three" is a chore you will do *sometimes* if the other person will also agree to do it sometimes. And "four" is something you just absolutely can't stand. After you've each ranked the items, get back together and compare lists.

"I'm always astonished at how the majority of chores seem to naturally sort themselves out," says Lasswell. Many times, for instance, people have clear preferences for different jobs ("I enjoy cooking, and you like doing the laundry"), or a clear desire to keep control of a given task. ("I want to be in charge of the kids' medical needs, and you like deciding where to invest our IRAs.")

You might want to keep several tips in mind during this divvying process. For one thing, do your best not to be bound by gender stereotypes for their own sake. In fact, you might even experiment with consciously swapping conventional male and female roles, at least occasionally. Let her mow the lawn; let him shop for the kids' clothes. Just knowing that your partner knows how to do all the different jobs of the household—and can be counted on to take over in a pinch—can be stress-relieving for both spouses.

Another thing to keep in mind is that even though mathematical equality is not necessarily the goal, you should take into account not only difficulty but the frequency factor of different tasks. Examples: Chauffeuring kids to sports games and recycling are usually rated relatively easy—though frequent—chores; dealing with repair people, cleaning the oven, and washing the inside and outside of windows, on the other hand, are more difficult but less regular activities. Again, you need to work out a system for handling these that feels good to all concerned.

It is probably also a good idea to try to divide up the "low control" tasks—that is, those jobs that absolutely must be done (feeding the children, handling emergency repairs). Because the person responsible for each "low control" job has little discretion in scheduling when it is done, these tasks tend to generate more stress than "high control" jobs (gardening, repainting the living room), which can be scheduled according to convenience.

Step 7. Involve the kids. All the steps enumerated so far apply as equally to children as they do to spouses or housemates. Beginning at age four or five or even younger, most children *want* to help, especially if they are given some encouragement to do so. "My stepdaughter was picking up everyone else's dirty clothes and putting them in the hamper when she was three," recalls one mother. "She absolutely loved doing it—and she did it very well."

The two biggest mistakes parents make are flip-sides of the same coin. The first occurs when parents *command* their children to do chores without giving them any say in the matter. When children balk—and most humans of any age treated like slaves do eventually balk—the exasperated parents often make the second mistake. That is, they go to the opposite extreme and simply do the task themselves.

Case in point: When her stepson was in junior high, a West Coast publisher found herself fighting almost every night over his assigned chore of doing the dishes. The lad had been delegated this task without any say on his part. He had begrudgingly agreed to do the chore before bed at 10:00 P.M., but he felt no real responsibility for it. Indeed, his behavior was pretty much what you might expect from someone chaffing under what he considered an authoritarian regime. Each night as the clock was just about to strike ten, he would race to the kitchen and fling the dishes into the dishwasher before racing to his bed.

Meanwhile, his stepmother was left seething. Often, he didn't make it to bed until 10:10—should she complain about this, or the fact that he forgot to soak the pots and pans? And what did "cleaning the dishes" really mean—did, for instance, the counter need to be empty to qualify?

"Sometimes I'd say something, sometimes not," the woman recalls years later. "I just hated being the enforcer, the nag. I would not do the dishes for him—I think four days of not doing them was his record. But I was furious every minute. And nothing was ever happily resolved about it. A dirty dish here and there is no big deal to me, but this was a major power struggle."

Power struggle, says Lasswell, is a good term to describe many chores situations gone sour. "When people get into a conflict of wills about chores, whether it's husbands and wives or parents and children, they will argue about everything. That's the nature of a power struggle—it makes cooperation impossible."

The remedy for chore wars with your kids is not so terribly different than the remedy for chore wars between spouses or roommates: Change the mindset from adversaries looking for loopholes to teammates looking for team solutions. And this means giving kids some say in what work they prefer to do. Lasswell recalls one family in which the eight-year-old daughter was resisting her parents' pleas for help around the house. The parents believed they were just being reasonable and that mandating a few chores, such as drying the dishes each night, was a good way to instill a work ethic in their daughter. The daughter, for her part, felt she was being treated like a slave. When Lasswell asked the daughter what chores she would like to do, the little girl replied, to her parent's astonishment, "Clean the bathroom."

"Oh, no," interjected the mother. "You're too young to do that."

Lasswell suggested the mother reserve judgment and give the

daughter a try. The result: a spotlessly cleaned bathroom every week. And as a reward for doing this job, Lasswell suggested—and the parents agreed—that she should be excused from drying the dishes each night, a chore the daughter said she loathed.

Ultimately, there is no right or wrong way to divide up the work, and every household will come up with different apportionments. What is critical, once again, is that all parties involved feel they have had a say in choosing their jobs and setting the standards, and all parties feel they are being treated fairly and with respect.

Step 8. Strive to have a good team—but don't demand a Dream Team. Those who hold the higher standards of cleanliness often find themselves wishing everyone else was more proficient at domestic work. In the best of all worlds, we might all have flashes of Martha Stewart, Dr. Spock, and Heloise within us. But in reality, the lion's share of us fall significantly below world-class status in *anything*, let alone housework. This is not to say that incompetence should be embraced or that anyone should be excused from learning and practicing the necessary skills. But it is to say that teams are more than the sum of their members, and that sometimes squads boasting the best individual athletes are trounced by much less gifted players who know how to work together.

Step 9. Tackle the supplemental list. As easy as you will probably find it to divide up a good portion of the chores, inevitably you must turn your attentions to the dreaded supplemental list—that final repository for all the items you can't agree on. Herein lie the hideous chores that none of you want to do—cleaning out the septic tank, perhaps, or washing the third-floor windows.

Never fear! For one thing, during the process of working together in good faith to apportion the master list, you will have both undoubtedly learned much about the art of being fair to one another. You may be surprised to find that you can quickly plink off a number of the chores that once seemed impossibly difficult to agree on. Not that each and every one will be easy to decide on. But again, if you find yourselves locking horns, try coming up with a compromise—and remember, there truly are myriad different options.

For example, if you have the money to hire the job out, it might make sense to do so. Or you can agree to write down the despicable job on a slip of paper and draw it from a hat—call this chores roulette. Perhaps you are willing to exchange one onerous task for two less onerous tasks, or maybe it makes sense to take turns on a rotating basis. ("I'll trap the rats in our basement *this* time—you do it next time.")

Sometimes even the more conscientious partner may come to realize that a given task is ultimately not all that important in the greater scheme of things. In such cases, you may well agree to do the task less often and less well. ("Let's not polish the silver until the next time royalty visits.")

But what if you find yourself locking horns over an item that one of you desperately wants done, but the other one sees absolutely no reason for doing at all? On the surface, there may seem to be only one solution—that is, the one who wants the job done may have to just do it. If the partner shouldering the task does not feel this is unfair, there's nothing wrong with simply settling the matter in this way. But often, says Lasswell, such a unilateral workload tips the scales toward a perceived unfairness.

A good way to compromise here is to come up with some kind of *quid pro quo* which may or may not involve other domestic work. Explains Lasswell: "Maybe the wife says to her husband, 'Look, I have wound up with ten things that you don't think need to be done, but that are very important to me. Is there some way that if I do some of these, you can help me with others? If you help me, maybe I will, in turn, do something that you'd like me to do—play golf with you on Saturday morning, or go see a science fiction movie with you.'" Kids are particularly motivated by *quid pro quos*—my son once straightened up our entire house, including his little brother's room, in exchange for a subscription to *National Geographic* magazine.

Step 10. Post the list where everyone can see it. Once you've divided everything up, pencil the tasks onto a monthly calendar and place this in some prominent spot, such as the refrigerator. You need to realize that the chores division is not etched in stone, but give the apportionment a trial for thirty days, agreeing ahead of time that you will reassess and make changes if necessary at the end of the month (or sooner if problems arise).

Ultimately, of course, the goal of any household task inventory and schedule is to make domestic work easier to get done. Whether you use an organizational software program, or low-tech pen and paper, you're creating a memory jogger to help make a positive change. But once again, it's only effective when you use this as a way to facilitate teamwork and cooperation—not as a kind of judicial consent decree each person is doing his or her best to worm out of.

Indeed, as the O'Tooles' experience suggests, problems are almost inevitable if households stop thinking of this as a tool, but rather start viewing it as a way of keeping score in an ongoing "tit for tat" debate. "On April 11th, the master schedule decreed you take the storm windows out and put the screen windows in—and you didn't do it till the 16th! I can't believe what a scofflaw you are." "Oh Yeah? Well, according to my records, you were supposed to mail the rent last Wednesday, and you waited till Friday, and now we're facing a forty-seven-cent service charge! Spendthrift!"

If you think this sounds a little ridiculous, consider the true-life marriage of two engineers in Albuquerque, New Mexico. Both spouses had already gone through divorces and were anxious to avoid future relationship problems. Their solution: an incredibly detailed prenuptial agreement that not only spelled out how their finances would be divided, but also defined exactly how they would live their lives together. Here are a few examples: The couple agreed to go to bed at 11:30 P.M. and rise at precisely 6:30 A.M.; he was in charge of paying bills and the maintenance of the outside of their home; she was in charge of household chores and grocery shopping, which she promised to accomplish by working from an agreed upon list; they would engage in healthy sex three to five times per week; neither one would ever leave anything on the floor overnight unless they were packing for a trip; the gas gauge in their car would never be allowed to fall below one-quarter; and so on, for sixteen detailed pages.

As each chore is completed by the family member who contracted to do it, check it off the calendar. Such a system, popular in day care centers and prisons, may seem hokey to grown adults, but it can prove surprisingly effective. Researchers at Brigham Young University and Colorado College looked at eighteen couples who agreed to try a "non-blaming, non-male-bashing" contract approach to sharing chores. The couples were told that they didn't have to strive for fifty-fifty equality—just try to reach a point that both considered fair. All eighteen couples wrote up contracts, which they were free to modify over time. After six months, most of these contracts were still posted on the refrigerators—and most of the men were still doing what they said they would.

Step 11. Incorporate a penalty clause. Cooperation works best if no one is forced to serve as the Big Policeman. If someone fails to do a job they agreed to do, it can be helpful to have a previously agreed upon consequence for this inaction. Maybe this means that the person will be automatically take on another duty, or that he or she must contribute some money to a family fund. But don't be too quick to invoke the penalty. Perhaps the job was left undone for a legitimate reason—an illness or an unexpected out-of-town business trip. Assume the best, not the worst, about your teammates, and remember, your ultimate goal is to pull in the same direction.

Step 12. Reward and reevaluate. Rats reinforced with a nice piece of rat kibble learn quickly how to perform desired tasks. We humans are not so different; reward yourselves with a nice dinner out, or give your child permission to buy a little treat he or she has wanted. (One important caution about rewards for adults, says Lasswell: Couples should *not* use sex as an incentive—or, for that matter, withdraw sex as a penalty—for chores behavior.)

Realize, too, that praise is a great motivator. Many young kids respond fantastically to checklists upon which an ever growing number of golden stars are applied for jobs well done. A well-timed word of praise, of course, can work miracles at any age. Consider: The French composer Jules Massenet was once conducting a rehearsal of one of his operas. The assembled chorus—a local choir—was lackluster at best. But he urged them on by saying, "Brother and sister artists! Sing as though the audience had applauded!" The appeal proved immediately successful.

The bottom line: Commend work others do do, even if it doesn't quite meet your own standards. And celebrate what has been accomplished instead of dwelling too much on the things left undone.

Finally, remember that ongoing communication is an essential aspect of teamwork. Lasswell recommends holding regular meetings at a minimum of once a month to discuss how the household is progressing. Obviously, if one or more family members undergo relapses or backsliding into old habits, you will need to meet more frequently. The most important element to remember is to work together in good faith. If someone is neglecting her agreed upon duties, don't go ballistic and treat her like a scofflaw. Talk things out with the goal of finding solutions. Try saying, for instance, something like this: "It looks like you are not doing this task. What's wrong? Do you still want this job, or do you want to look at the list and pick another one?"

Housemate Situations: Special Concerns

The same basic strategies that can help couples and families organize and allocate household chores can also work with roommates. The main difference is that you usually don't *love* your roommates, indeed, you might not even *like* them unless you have purposely chosen to share a house with friends. In most big cities where rents are skyrocketing, many roommates are essentially strangers thrown together out of economic necessity.

This, of course, has both a downside and an upside. The downside is that there is no love between you as a baseline motivator for cooperation. The upside is that if things get too bad, you can always just walk out—a virtually guiltless option for roommates, but one that has excruciating consequences for family members.

Suzanne Friedman, whose housesharing referral service on the West Coast helps match thousands of roommates each year, cautions her clients to do their homework before moving into shared housing. "If you have a bad job, at least you can go home to get away from it. But if you have a bad living situation, there's no escape," says Friedman, who has conducted seminars on communal living.

Friedman and a host of veteran housemates recommend the following steps, which boil down to cautiously sizing up any situation *before* you decide to move in, then instituting rituals that encourage regular communication and a fair alternation of the common work. Especially if you are new to the process of communal living, you might want to keep these points in mind:

True Compatibility Is More Than Just Politics

When house members interview a prospective roommate, they tend to ask about hobbies, tastes in music, smoking preferences, politics, and the like. "But," says a former roommate who moved in with young adults who initially seemed like her long-lost spiritual soul mates, "whether someone is an award-winning racquetball player who practices the teachings of Ghandi really doesn't matter much if they aren't also willing to mop the floor once a month."

Interview the Interviewers

Remember that while the housemates are sizing you up, you should also be sizing them up. Since they have a vested interest in getting someone to move in and share the rent, odds are they will be on their best behavior. Look around the house, check behind closed doors, investigate the pantry and laundry room. Chances are the housemates have tried their best to clean the place up to impress you, and chances are it will *never* be appreciably neater than it is right now.

Friedman, for her part, believes that getting references is a good idea, too. "But go back at least two prior landlords," she says. "Sometimes a landlord will give a real deadbeat a great reference just to get rid of them." Ask about employment, too, and later check with the employers to verify what they tell you is true. Amazing as this may seem, failure to pay rent is not, in some states, sufficient grounds for evicting a tenant. You definitely don't want to get stuck paying the rent for a roommate who's fallen on hard (or lazy) times.

Ask What the House Rules Are

If cleanliness and order are important to you, your odds of finding a personally tolerable situation are much higher if the existing roommates already have some sort of plan for sharing the work. If you're told that people "just sort of pitch in" as needed, chances are the place is going to be pretty messy most of the time. Ask how often and well the bathroom is cleaned, ask how often the place is dusted and floors mopped, ask about all the nitty-gritty house chores that are important to you. Ask also how they handle kitchen duties—does everyone cook their own meals, and if so, is there any policy about cleaning up the kitchen so another roommate is not left with dirty pans and dishes to clean before he or she can start his or her own meal preparation? "It may sound ridiculous," says Friedman, "but when you live day-to-day with other people, these issues really matter."

Ask about the Pet Policy

Pets can definitely contribute to household mess. "Some people," says Friedman, "think that birds are very benign, but they can really carry on in the early morning." Add to this noise the scattering of bird seed and the byproducts thereof across the floor. Dog and cat hairs, not to mention pet "accidents," can require a lot of household maintenance. If you like pets, great—just make sure all the roommates are on the same wavelength. "There really should be no unilaterals when it comes to animals," says Friedman.

Standards Cut Both Ways

Be honest with yourself about your own feelings. If you're *not* a neatnik, moving into a house filled with them may seem like a great way to get a gaggle of maids for free. The reality, however, is that fastidious souls will make a lone slob feel just as miserable as the vice versa situation. The bottom line: Seek mess-compatible housemates and avoid the potential for friction and resentments.

Look for Open Communicators

There are always going to be tensions when humans live together, but these tensions can be dissipated through communication and problem solving. The alternative, of course, is to say nothing—and let minor irritations fester into hellish dimensions that dramatically erode the quality of daily living. "Everyone has their non-negotiables," says one happy housemate. "You have to be very honest about your levels of cleanliness and task-sharing, and you have to get these out in the open immediately."

Insist on a Month-by-Month Lease

Until you've had a while to actually live with your new roommates, it's going to be hard to predict what the chemistry between you will be. Don't agree to a long-term lease—you will feel much better psychologically if you know you can beat a hasty retreat if things don't work out.

Once You're In, Ritualize Cooperation

Some of the larger roommate referral services across the country have tried to make it easier for renters to find roommates with similar housekeeping and task-sharing standards. Many services, for instance, use a chore wheel, which assigns different tasks on a rotating basis. It works like this: On a center wheel, groupings of chores are written down in sections resembling slices of pie. On a moveable outer wheel, the roommate's names are each written. Every day, this outer wheel turns a notch—and the roommates each have a new day's chore assignments.

Whether your household uses a chore wheel or some other method of assigning housework, you have to agree to hold up your end before you move in. In your household, you may find it preferable to share tasks according to the different talents and predilections of the house members. If there's a gourmet cook in your midst, for instance, you might want to trade some cleaning duties for a great group dinner once a week. Or perhaps you might all agree to chip in and hire a housecleaner on a regular basis. No matter what method of allocating chores you decide on, you should incorporate a penalty clause for failure to do contracted assignments. This could be anything from doing an unpopular chore (cleaning the bathroom) or contributing an agreed upon amount of money into the household coffers (perhaps to pay a maid or to cover the expenses of a party).

One final note on chores allocation: Even if you and your housemates decide not to rotate tasks, it's probably a good idea that everyone in the house have the experience of performing each task at least once. "That way," says Friedman, "everyone will at least know what work is involved. If for no other reason, it's important to know how to do these jobs so that you can take over in a pinch."

Keep on Discussing Things

Schedule a house meeting no less than once a month to talk over how the household is operating. In order for your house to run without rancor, everyone must have a fair say in setting standards and deciding how tasks are allocated. Just as with couples, you will almost certainly have to compromise and meld your values with everyone else's. *Don't* expect things to go exactly your way; *do* expect your roommates to meet your standards part way. As long as you keep discussing the household openly—and you make adjustments when necessary—your relationship with your roommates has a good chance of smooth sailing.

Your Room is Your Castle

Housekeeping rules and standards should apply to all common spaces, from the living room and hallways to the kitchen and bath. Each housemate's private room, however, is and should remain their own inner sanctum, a place to keep neat, or not, as they see fit. The only exception to this is if the room somehow impacts the rest of the house. Health code violations, for instance, or loud stereo music late at night, clearly shouldn't be tolerated. But as long as the way a housemate chooses to live inside his or her room does not impinge on the others, you should definitely strive to adopt a *laissez-faire* attitude.

Consider an Intervention

Oftentimes, the majority of roommates can be quite diligent about their responsibilities at home, while one member slacks off. If peer pressure is not enough to get this person to contribute his or her fair share, Friedman recommends a gentle, positive intervention.

"Your goal is not to scare or berate this other person," she says, "but to modify their behavior. Try saying something like this: 'We really enjoy living with you, but we need to work out a few things. We are tired, for instance, of having to be bill collectors each month to get your share of the rent. And we are also tired of being your parent and picking up after you.'"

A Few Notes on Delegating

Whether you're in a housemate situation or in a committed relationship, it's probably a mistake for the person who has traditionally been in charge of the household to imagine that any schedule or chore wheel will magically remove *all* need for delegating. Indeed, many women in charge of the homefront report that they don't want to completely share authority. If you and your mate prefer a copresidency, fine—more power to you. But in many cases, one person will probably find himself having to remind others to do a chore—or at the very least, remind him to look at the schedule.

If you go into this with the idea that scheduling chores is the ultimate panacea for all chore wars problems, you're probably asking for disappointment. Instead, try to see the schedule as a tool which, over time, will help establish patterns that become at least somewhat habitual (and thus less likely to require as much reminding). Here are some other tips from psychologists and home economists for how the major homemaker can delegate effectively:

- Don't be a superwoman—if you shoulder all the work yourself, there will be nothing left for the rest of the family to do. In an interesting variation on the Nike slogan, sometimes it's important to remind yourself: Just don't do it.

- Don't be ambivalent about asking other family members to do their share. Maybe you feel on some level that these jobs really are your responsibility alone. This is crazy. Sharing work is good for everyone—it keeps you from becoming overly stressed, it teaches your kids a work ethic that will serve them well all their lives, and it lets your spouse become a more full participant in life at home.

- Don't expect your family members to be superman, supergirl, superboy, or, for that matter, superdog. Life today is extremely hectic for most of us, and it's important to have reasonable standards. As much as you might like to have the multicourse family meals you remember from childhood, for instance, you might have to make do with takeout or boil-in-the-bag microwave foods a few times a week. Remember: It is possible to cook fast and eat healthfully.

- Sometimes, it might seem easier to just do a given job yourself, or that for the sake of keeping the peace, you ought to just do it. Perhaps short term this might actually be correct—but you have to think long term. Remember: Your loved ones will never become competent self-starters if they aren't given ample opportunities to practice. Again, remember each time you're tempted to steal such opportunities away: Just don't do it.

- If a member of the household neglects to do a job he has agreed to do, don't assume the worst—that is, that the deadbeat is a pathological slacker whose only purpose in life is to drive you crazy. Give him a reasonable amount of time to get the job done, and if it still is not completed after this interlude, *remind* him. Remember, people tend to rise to the level of your expectations—if you assume your husband, for instance, is a weasel, chances are he'll become one eventually. If, on the other hand, you figure he's a great guy who just hasn't had a chance to fulfill his obligation, chances are he'll get around to it soon.

- Don't plead or nag for help—not only does this put you into the Big Boss role, it also puts your spouse, kids, or housemates into the less-than-thrilled employee role.

- On the other hand, it's okay to explain *how* to do a job, especially if the other person solicits your advice. Be specific—don't tell a child, for instance, to clean the kitchen—ask her to rinse the dishes off and place them in the dishwasher. To be sure she understands you, you can ask her to repeat back what you've just said.

- Play zone defense—each household member is responsible for his own private space, bedroom, home office, or what have you. Let him keep his given zones as clean—or as messy—as he wants, as long as it doesn't endanger the rest of the family (mold; fire hazards) or intrude into common space (toy proliferation spilling out into the hallway).

- When problems arise, don't wait until you're so mad you explode. Instead, set aside a calm time for a household meeting.

- Consider farming out some of the work—for instance, hiring a maid for occasional heavy cleaning, a neighborhood kid to mow your grass, or a window washer to do outside windows. To pay for such services, ask each family member to economize by giving up one expense he or she normally incurs. Maybe this means brown-bagging lunch instead of eating out or renting fewer videos. Make sure everyone has a share in paying for jobs that benefit the whole family.

- Many merchants provide free pickup and delivery service—you can eliminate many time-consuming errands by taking advantage of such services. In some areas, you can even grocery shop via phone, fax, or e-mail.

- Try to have everyone adopt some basic habits that will reduce the amount of work that's necessary to do. Get into the habit of taking off muddy shoes by the door and don't let clutter accumulate—file it or toss it.

- If all else fails, go on strike. This is the ultimate *just don't do it* stratagem, but it can be surprisingly effective. Not only are you likely to be surprised by how much and how quickly the rest of the household will pitch in, you will also find that your nightmare of a dysfunctional garbage house was at least somewhat exaggerated.

When to Seek Help

If you have tried the various self-help approaches recommended in this book and you're still having major problems over chore wars, you might want to seek help from a qualified therapist. If you have car problems, you go to an auto mechanic. If you have legal problems, you see a lawyer. It is the same with problems at home—sometimes an outside expert can really help families who are stuck in patterns they can't budge on their own.

If you are interested in getting help, you can often find a good therapist by asking your friends who have gone to counseling. You can also get a referral by writing to the American Association for Marriage and Family Therapy, 1133 15th Street NW, Suite 300, Washington, D.C., or by calling (800) 992-2638 or (202) 452-0190.

Chapter 6

TEACH YOUR CHILDREN WELL

Ensuring Peace for the Next Generation

The more people have studied different methods of bringing up children, the more they have come to the conclusion that what good mothers and fathers instinctively feel like doing for their babies is the best after all.
　　　　　—Dr. Benjamin Spock

Children aren't happy with nothing to ignore, and that's what parents were created for.
　　　　　—Ogden Nash

I tried to raise my son, now twenty-seven, to be a sensitive new age kinda guy. But two years ago, when he called me to tell me he was getting married, I asked him to tell me about his wife-to-be. He said, "She's just great, Mom. She does my dishes and cleans my apartment." I wanted to die. So much for my efforts. The way to a man's heart is still through his Dustbuster.
　　　　　—Jane T.

My wife was raised to believe life is business; life is errands; life is getting things done. I want to raise our kid to do stupid things—tumble down the steps, stick his foot in his mouth, lick ice cream from the bowl. I want him to have a stupid, goofy childhood. My mother-in-law would prefer that a two year old act like a twenty year old.
　　　　　—Andy K.

Mary Ellen's Story

"When our son and daughter were very young, household work used to be much more of a source of stress and resentment for me than it is now. I used to think everything had to be kept to the same standards I had before the kids were born. Back then, my husband, Tom, and I would spend one day a week thoroughly cleaning our house.

"Slowly, however, I have tried to make peace with the fact that there's no way the house can be kept the way I would ideally want it to be—there are just too many other things going on in our lives. Just keeping track of the family can sometimes be overwhelming—for example, who needs to go to the dentist, orthodontist, eye doctor, and so on; who needs new clothes, shoes, glasses; who needs to be picked up and delivered, and where and when, and so forth ad infinitum. 'Optional' jobs like cleaning out the front hall closet may still be done regularly—but regularly may mean once every two years.

"The firestorm of kid-oriented details can really clutter the brain, but these have to be scheduled into our lives by someone. I think Tom and I basically do the best that we can. We need more hours in the day.

"Both my husband and I are consciously trying to teach our kids how to do a little bit of everything on the homefront, from cooking to laundry to cleaning. That way, at least they'll have the basic skills down when they get on their own. They have seen their Dad do just about everything in the house, so I don't think they'll have quite the same gender-defined roles as we did growing up.

"Having said this, getting the kids to work around the house still requires constant reminding. My son is twelve now, and he's a bit of an entrepreneur. He'll volunteer to do beyond-the-call-of-duty special cleaning projects, provided we pay him. When he is low on cash, he is a great help. Otherwise, it can be difficult, at best, to enlist his efforts. I don't know if it's genetic or socialization or what, but my daughter is generally a lot more likely to pitch in on her own. And she's only seven.

"Sometimes I fear that despite all our efforts, my son will drive his future wife crazy because she will constantly have to be after him to do anything. And he'll just expect things to be done for him. And my daughter has told me she doesn't want to work outside the home the way I do. She's just a first grader, and I hope that between now and when she's older she'll reconsider. But she's told me that she sees all the stress in my life, and her attitude right now is: 'Why would I want to go through what you go through?' "

Tom's Story

"I definitely want my son and daughter to know how to take care of themselves when they leave for college or wherever. We're not going to be around to cook and wash their clothes. We have them do some chores occasionally now—probably more would be better. But at least they get enough practice so that they'll know how to do it when they have to.

"I hope Mary Ellen knows how much the kids and I appreciate what she does for us. Sometimes I worry about how tired my wife gets—in my view, she does more for the children and the house and me than she needs to. I talk to her about it and try to persuade her to let go of some of the work and take more time for herself—fun, self-indulgent time. I think I'm making headway—she has been telling the kids 'no' a little more often than in the past.

"There are still occasions when I am too busy to pitch in at all. Last Christmas, for instance, I was swamped with work, and my mother was in the hospital dying from cancer. One night I came up a little shell-shocked from my design studio in the basement of our house. It was well after midnight, and I'd been working all day. What I saw in the living room stunned me—the Christmas tree was decorated and lit up, the mantle above the fireplace was decorated, and there was a winter village set up in another corner of the living room.

"The house was perfectly still, my wife and our kids were already sleeping. I just stood there, amazed at what I was seeing. The work she did filled our home with the holiday spirit. My children and I will never forget it.

"I am very aware of the role modeling my wife and I are doing for our kids. I would like to think that my son, by seeing a father who does do some household chores, will not enter his own marriage the way I did— that is, with a profound insensitivity and lack of consciousness about these issues. Early in our marriage, chore wars were a constant source of stress and resentment for Mary Ellen and me. We both were raised in traditional Ozzie-and-Harriet type homes, and it took me a long time—and pain—to realize that this is no way to live when both adults have full-time jobs. It's very important to me that I pass down to my son a different set of values, so that when he gets married he doesn't get whacked in the head the way I feel I did with, 'Hey, this is the world. Wake up!'

"I also find myself praying that our daughter does decide to pursue both family and a career. I feel very strongly about this—she has a terrific role model in her mother. And I see how much of Mary Ellen's self-image and self-esteem stems from her career. I think that is a tremendous thing to pass on to our daughter—that women can have more than just one role. I would feel very bad if she doesn't pick up on this message."

Removing Gender from Housework

One of the main reasons so many working couples today wage chore wars is because almost all of us—men and women—were raised in era that reinforced the idea that some kinds of work were to be done by men and some kinds by women. Perhaps the best hope to save the next generation from repeating our own domestic stresses is to somehow begin to degenderize household work.

If you have kids, chances are you have more housework than ever, and much less time to do it. No doubt you've also become thoroughly acquainted with the Second Law of Thermodynamics. That's the one that deals with entropy and the fact that energy runs perpetually down hill. Put another way, a Lego pirate ship, painstakingly assembled over the course of several hours, will eventually disassemble into tiny pieces of multicolored plastic strewn throughout every nook and cranny of your house.

"We're much more organized, better housecleaners than when we first met," says Henry, a programmer, who's been married to Rachel, a nurse, for fourteen years. "But our house is much worse. How can this be? Can you say c-h-i-l-d-r-e-n?"

On the plus side, the arrival of kids often forces couples to alter their no longer realistic standards, and there's a certain liberating quality in this. As most parents discover soon enough, children are an irrepressible force of nature, not unlike ocean waves that turn a rocky cliff into a sandy beach. Kids demand that their parents get their priorities straight, and who can argue with them? Who among us really believes, for instance, that a perfectly clean house is more important than trying to comfort a child who has had a bad day at school?

This doesn't mean that parents can or should open the flood gates to complete household chaos. And it doesn't mean that parents alone should undertake all the work of running the house. In many ways, it helps to think of the extra work as a good thing in that it provides your kids with ample opportunities to master skills and take responsibility for the household they, too, inhabit and shape.

Teaching kids to do chores, and insisting they do them, may be one of the most important lessons both parents can provide. Studies, for instance, have suggested that kids who are expected to do chores also do better in school, possibly because the work ethic they learn in the house translates into a work ethic in academics.

Though some women remain reluctant to yield too much parenting responsibility to their husbands, and some men still think of fatherhood as a form of baby-sitting, such anachronistic attitudes appear to be diminishing. A generation or two ago, Ernest Hemingway hardly raised eyebrows with his first rule of successful fatherhood: "When you have a kid, don't look at it for the first two years." To be sure, if he were to make the same remark today, there's a legion of us dads who would be tempted to drop the old man into the sea.

Indeed, researchers who look at the role of fathers in their children's lives are finding that our active participation is essential to their future success. One scientist, for instance, who analyzed four generations of men found that fathers who helped their kids athletically, emotionally, and academically gave them a great advantage not only in school but in their future careers. Such benefits were not entirely one-sided either. In contrast to the idea that men must be fixated solely on their jobs to excel, actively participating fathers not only had happier marriages but better career success than their traditional, job-addicted, and worka-holic peers.

Preparing the Next Generation of Boys—and Girls—for an Egalitarian World

If the prospect of happy, successful adult kids isn't enough to convince both parents to fully participate in their young lives, consider this. Think of all the chore wars unhappiness you both have felt at times, and ask yourselves: Do I really want my son or daughter to have to relive this misery, too?

Degenderizing housework, of course, is a formidable task, and many social scientists would argue that total elimination of sexual roles is not only impossible but undesirable. Consider that sometime around the age of three, boys and girls begin to realize that they are, well, boys and girls, and this difference is going to be lifelong. Many (but not all) cultures reinforce these differences by according "men's work" a higher status than "women's work."

Ironically, the actual work itself is often secondary to its gender status. According to writer Mary Stewart Van Leeuwen, anthropologists have looked at two primitive cultures whose geographical territories border each other. In one tribe, basket weaving is considered low-class women's work, whereas house building is high-class men's work. In the adjacent culture, these classifications are completely reversed. Men in the second tribe take on the lofty job of basket weaving—and women undertake the lowly task of house building.

Though none of us are totally immune to the imperatives of our biology, neither are we wholly impotent to influence it. Van Leeuwen has found that there are cultures where the gender differences, though still very real, are nonetheless much downplayed by men and women alike. The Pygmies of Central Africa, for instance, live as small, tight-knit groups of hunter-gatherers. Survival depends on both sexes' working together for the common good. Grandfathers and grandmothers, for instance, both care for toddlers while both mother and father are out hunting.

The post-industrial economy of the United States in the 1990s and beyond may seem at first a far cry from the life of egalitarian Pygmies. But on closer reflection, our lives are perhaps not so different after all. For many of us, a single hunter-gatherer acting alone (like many of our own fathers) is no longer capable of bringing in the sustenance the family needs. Consider that an estimated 58 percent of mothers with small children are in the workforce.

Pygmy fathers share responsibility for their children because Pygmy mothers can't do it all. Necessity, for them and for many of us, begets a much more gender-neutral approach. The good thing is that boys and girls are great learners—when they see their parents working together, they learn that this is what good parents do. A lot can change in a single generation—and ours is arguably squarely on the pivot point.

If you need further proof that change is coming, consider this interesting datum: The *New York Times* recently reported that the percentage of boys in home economics classes nationwide has risen from 4.2 percent in 1968 to 41.5 percent today. And the 1993 President of the Future Homemakers of America was—you guessed it, a boy.

Psychologists tell us that kids learn their attitudes more from what we do than what we say. So dads, if you want your sons to be the father and husband you'd like to be yourself, don't just tell them to help their mom—show them by your actions that you are taking responsibility for the house, too.

And moms, if you want to save your daughters from being slaves to their own internal, oppressive, and unrealistic standards of perfection, show them by your own example that it's possible to find a good enough standard. And teach them how to change the oil!

Let your desire to change them be a prime motivator to change you.

Start Young

The earlier you begin expecting your children to take an active role in the household, the easier you will find it is to get them to comply. Many experts suggest that by the age of three or four, most kids are ready to handle small, age-appropriate work—putting away groceries, for instance, or setting and clearing the table. Remember, though, that their attention spans are short, and it's unreasonable to expect very young kids to work for more than a few minutes at a time.

Undoubtedly, there will be many occasions when it seems much easier to just do these tasks yourself rather than insisting a dawdling little one do it. But resist this impulse and try to be patient instead! It may, in fact, be easier and quicker now—but you are making a long-term investment in your child's competence and self-reliance.

Many kids respond well to checklists and colorful stickers to signify a job well done. Remember: Chores don't have to be drudgery—whenever possible, make a game of them.

Here are some chores experts suggest you can reasonably expect your children to handle at different ages:

- Three and four year olds can pick up their toys, straighten up their rooms, set the table (better to use plastic plates at this age), put their clean clothes into drawers, and water plants inside and out. There is hardly a kid in creation who doesn't enjoy sprinkling with a hose.

- Kids in kindergarten up through the fourth or fifth grade can learn to make their own beds, feed and walk the family dog, rinse dirty dishes and then put them in the dishwasher, sort and fold laundry, and dispose of the trash. At the latter end of this age range, many youngsters are eager for new responsibilities—teach them how to use the washer and dryer and show them how to cook simple meals with the microwave.

- By the time your children are on the cusp of adolescence, they're capable of fairly in-depth housecleaning—from dusting to floor mopping to vacuuming. They should, at this point, take responsibility for keeping their own rooms clean and learn how to do the entire laundry process, from initial sorting, to washing and drying, to folding and putting clothes away. Pre- and early teens are capable of outside work, too—shoveling snow and cutting the grass, for instance. Depending on the individual child, many kids this age are ready to do baby-sitting and other short-term care of younger siblings. One tip: Resist the urge to be sexist when allocating these jobs: Despite its name, a Lawn Boy should not be the sole province of boys; nor should babysitting fall automatically to the girls.

- Before you know it, your kids will have their learner's permits and be only a small step away from the adult world. For many teenagers fifteen and older, chores are likely to be the last things on their minds, and certainly it would be a mistake to treat your progeny as the long-lost maid/indentured servant you always wished you could afford. On the other hand, if you don't expect them to undertake some adult-level responsibilities, they're going to pay for it once they're on their own. By this age, there is very little your kids can't do around the house, from driving to the store for groceries to learning how to paint and undertake household repairs. This is also a great time to teach cooking, a skill that will almost certainly win them friends when they're on their own.

From Tot to Team Player

All this *sounds* great, you're probably telling yourself. But if your kids are still little engines of entropy like ours, you're probably also wondering how in the world such a transformation will *ever* happen. One quick glance around your living room seems to make this vision of responsible, self-reliant, nearly adult children a cruel and impossible dream.

To wit, your family room looks like a toy box just blew up in it— Monopoly money, Shark Attack pieces, Barbie clothes, coloring books, and the like are everywhere the reddened eye can roam. The same kids who did *this* will be driving to the store to pick up groceries a few years hence?

Get, as your seven year old tells you so frequently, *real!*

As important as it is to start kids doing chores young, it's also fiendishly difficult. But teach a lad how to straighten a room now, and all your subsequent lessons will be that much easier. Here's how some parents and experts alike recommend that you can get cooperative, cheerful help from recalcitrant rug rats:

Do It Together

Kids are more likely to clean up if they have company, and it gives you an opportunity to model behavior and to train them how to do the job. Get right down on the floor with them, advises Lexi Hoffman, a parent education/child development specialist in Hampton Falls, New Hampshire. Start putting the Monopoly pieces back in the box, and let them join you. Expect to repeat yourself, and to train and retrain.

Make It Fun

One of the easiest ways to bring joy to drudge work is to use music. "We sing a little song," says Maria Jenkins, director of the Giving Tree

Montessori School in Knoxville, Tennessee. The lyrics may sound hokey, but they work: "It's cleanup time. It's cleanup time. Please put your work away!"

As a joke, one father in New York City put on a record of college football marches during a family cleanup. He found that it worked, and now he plays the record all the time. The kids think its funny, he says, but the house gets cleaned up.

Another father from San Mateo, California, makes picking up fun by appealing to his to four year old's imagination "Oh, no—Mr. Crayon is lost and lonely!" he cries. "He needs to find his way back into the crayon box!" It doesn't take long for his son to join right in: "Oh, you naughty car!" he'll warn. "Get back in your garage right now!"

Offer Encouragement and Don't Nit-Pick

The coffee table may not be ready for a visit from the queen, but your child still deserves a hug or a pat on the back for making the effort. (Attentive readers will recall that this same advice works on husbands as well as tots.)

Break It Up

A two year old may love to take a doll and put it in its right place. A three year old may be able to put two books on a shelf, or put Legos in a box. But young children get frustrated with a messy room with too many unclear tasks.

Most jobs can be broken down into steps a child can master one at a time. Don't say, "Clean up this room." Say instead, "Put the action figures in a basket. Then, put the coloring books in the cubby. Then, put the pieces of trash in a trash bag."

Make a Place for Everything

It's no accident that child-care centers like to give everything a container (a box, basket, or tray), and a colored label that corresponds to a place on a shelf. Kids love to put things into boxes or crates. Then they can put the crates back on the shelf. Not only is this process fun for kids, but researchers looking at the cognitive development of young children have found such simple sorting can help lay a ground work for success in understanding more complex math.

Set a Time of the Day

Kids love routine. If your children know they'll be picking up their toys every evening after dinner and before the bath, they can get used to the idea and know what to expect. And once picking up becomes a habit, you'll have won the battle entirely.

Blitz!

When you need to straighten up the house fast (Grandma just called and she's on her way over!), try this strategy. Gather the whole family together and set the kitchen timer for a *short* time—five minutes, max. Then all of you launch yourselves on an energetic frenzy of picking up. One behavioral pediatrician has dubbed this the "White Tornado." Kids are happy to pitch in because it's competitive, fun, and, most importantly, there is a definite end in sight.

Ask, Don't Demand

Even among younger children, it makes a difference how you express yourself. If you *tell* a child to pick up a book, you're almost inviting them to say no. It might be different story if you ask for their help, which makes a child feel needed and valued.

Name the Job, Not the Child

Describe what you need to have done (for instance, "I want those books put back on the shelves"), rather than evaluating the child's behavior or character. Avoid saying such things as, "Look at this place! How could you make such a mess! Why can't you ever keep this room neat?"

Use One Word

Rather than launching on a dissertation any time you want something picked up, keep it simple. Have you ever met a kid who wants to hear a lecture? Say: "Books!" or "Games!" or "Wet towels!" The pithy approach communicates without criticizing or expressing all the anger and annoyance you might be feeling. It also encourages your child to find out the solution for himself or herself. A variation of this technique is to leave short notes on problem areas. New readers, especially, enjoy the idea that someone has written them a note.

Use Positive Reinforcement, not Bribery

Try to stay away from rewards, as such, for regular, everyday cleanup. Compliment the child for completing a job, but avoid succumbing to bargaining tactics like, "I'll clean up *if* you take me to the movies afterwards."

Make Boredom as Your Ally

If a child refuses to cooperate with cleanup, it generally does more harm than good to force the issue. The most common result is to harden a child's resolve. It's smarter for a parent to calmly explain that there will be no Nintendo or TV until after cleanup. This strategy is a little like judo—rather than being directly confrontational, you're allowing the force of the child's own boredom to steer them in the right direction.

From Learners to Performers: Tackling the Teenage Transition

For parents determined to help their children become competent self-starters on the homefront, the pre-teen and teenage years represent a tremendous challenge—a transitional period where children and parents alike must necessarily undergo striking changes in how they relate to one another. Says Molly Fumia, author of *Honor Thy Children*, and herself the mother of six (three current teenagers, two former teenagers, and one soon-to-be teenager), "There remains an inherent relational conflict between parent and child during these years of adolescence. On the one hand, the child is striving for independence from his or her parents, a goal that most parents, at least intellectually, want to encourage."

On the other hand, many parents feel an obligation, sometimes bordering on frenzy, to instill greater responsibility in their teenager. The tools they may have used when the child was younger often boiled down to parental decrees. Hence the dilemma: How can you *mandate* a son or daughter do a chore—in essence, treating them like a child—but at the same time affirm in them the fact that they are becoming independent, take-charge individuals for whom coercion is not a necessary precondition of chores performance?

"I think it's critical," says Fumia, "that you keep your eyes on the *real* prize, which is to help foster within your teenager a sense of independence, self-reliance, and feelings of responsibility to others in the community. This is a *much* more important goal than just ensuring, for instance, that they get their socks in the hamper. I'm not suggesting that chores are unimportant—I am suggesting that parents need to use a different approach than the one that may have worked during childhood to encouraging teens. Any parent who tries to control a teen the way they controlled a six year old is almost sure to find it just doesn't work. I know there are some parents who will disagree with me, but I believe parental demands and punishment do nothing to teach responsibility—they only encourage teenagers to become experts at finding loopholes."

Judy Ford, author of *Wonderful Ways to Love a Teen,* agrees that the real challenge of fostering responsibility in your teenager is to find ways to make his inner quest for adulthood—rather than your orders—his main motivation for action. "Understand that the goal is not to get the child to do X because you've decreed it," explains Ford, the mother of a seventeen-year-old daughter. "The goal is to help teenagers to find satisfaction from within themselves, satisfaction that comes from pitching in, being responsible, making a contribution, and taking a real sense of pride in the space they share with others. Realize that in a very real sense, they shouldn't be doing chores to please their parents, but to please themselves. You are tapping into their own inner motivation to do the right thing."

Making this shift from parenting a child who needs guidance and a certain amount of dictatorial directives to parenting a teenager who needs to learn to function autonomously can be very hard on parents. "The biggest fights you have over chores," says Ford, "are often fueled by a parent's fear and grief about having to let go. Parents suddenly become aware that their child, in whose life they have been involved in every aspect, now has a life the parent may know nothing about. This freaks parents out, triggering deep grieving that, in turn, really gets the battles going."

Because of this, both Ford and Fumia suggest, change must be a two-way street. "If you as a parent want to emerge from this very difficult passage having a good relationship with your kids," explains Fumia, "it means you are going to have to change, too. Don't expect the teenage years to be easy—I don't know anyone, parent or kid, who has had an easy time of it. But it's all so worthwhile and satisfying when your kids do leave home and immediately demonstrate they can take responsibility for their own lives."

Against this philosophical framework of helping your teen become a responsible adult, Fumia, Ford, and other experts recommend some practical tips for coping with and encouraging the transition:

Embrace the Change

Realize it's normal and healthy for teens to make a psychological separation from their parents. It's also normal for you to feel ambivalence about this—you are, in a real sense, losing your kids to their own imminent adulthood. Despite such grieving, remember the consequences of *not* letting them go. "Do you really want them to live with you forever, helpless and dependent on your care?" asks Ford. Such a question can go a long way toward focusing your mind in the right direction.

Their Room Is Their Castle

Let your teen keep her room any way she wishes, assuming this doesn't violate any local statutes. When her daughter was seven, Ford made a rule that as long as there was an open path through strewn toys to the little girl's bed, it was okay. Later Ford added a codicil: The daughter had to be able to close her door, too, so that the atmosphere of chaos would not percolate out to the rest of the house. As the daughter grew older, Ford began laying groundwork for her daughter's future sense of personal responsibility. " 'I am really looking forward,' " she would tell her, 'to the day when you can clean up your room.' I tried to be very patient, and I mean years of patience. I didn't scream and yell—I bit my tongue." Ford's strategy eventually paid off big time. At the age of fourteen, her daughter—without any prompting—returned from school one day and cleaned her room. Since that occasion, her room has consistently been the cleanest and neatest in the whole house. "I really believe," says Ford, "that by allowing her to keep her room the way she wanted to, my daughter had an opportunity to 'explore messiness' and to ultimately decide this was not the way she wanted to live. I can't know for certain, but I do believe that if I had forced the issue, she may have permanently embraced messiness as a way of defying my orders."

You Set the Standards for Shared Spaces

Do set ground rules for common spaces, ground rules that must be honored by your teens and their friends. "I've always insisted," says Ford, "that all kids coming into my house take off their shoes at the front door. My house is my temple, and I like to keep it very neat. The kids are free to laugh and have fun, of course, but they have learned to treat our home with respect. If they want to jump on furniture, they can go to a friend's house where this is okay. But in our house, they walk with respect."

Don't Label Your Teen Lazy or a Slacker

Some parents are very quick to blame any less-than-perfect chores performance. But by doing this, parents are just using chores as yet another excuse for a family fight. Instead, try to see chores as a great opportunity to help adolescents learn the skills of cooperation and negotiation. "I really believe that teenage kids who are sloppy are not doing this to be mean," explains Fumia. "They're doing it because their sense of responsibility has not caught up with the rest of them. When one of my sons leaves his clothes on the floor, I'd always ask him, 'Are you leaving those for the maid?' It took him a while, but he eventually understood that the consequences of his inaction were that someone else—usually me—had to pick up his clothes for him. Your goal is getting the teenager to know it's his responsibility. The other day, my son saw me coming and he raced over to pick up his socks. 'Don't worry, Mom,' he told me. 'I didn't leave these for the maid.'"

If You Want a Teenager to Lose His or Her Attitude, Try Losing *Yours* First

Some parents subscribe to a kind of modern day Calvinism that says teenagers *need* to suffer drudgery at home, because enduring drudgery for its own sake is character-building. Such an attitude is extremely counterproductive. Instead, when you do chores yourself, try doing them as cheerfully as possible. "I really subscribe to the Zen philosophy that says there's joy in chopping wood and carrying water," says Ford. "In our family, finding shared joy in everyday tasks is one of the things that makes our family life so rich." Adds Fumia: "Remember that the way you act role models how you want them to act. It's amazing how effective a little generosity of spirit on your part can help your kids learn to be generous themselves."

Let a Son or Daughter's Innate Interest In domestic Jobs Motivate Him or Her

Beginning in the fourth grade, one pre-teen girl told her parents that she wanted to start doing her own laundry. At first, her mother balked—her daughter was simply too young for such a job. Better, at this age, to take out the garbage. But the daughter persisted, and eventually she won her mother over. She has done a perfect job ever since her first load midway through her fourth grade year. In another family, the eleven-year-old son loved to look at the photographs of gourmet foods in his mother's cook books. So she started buying him a lavishly illustrated cookbook of his own each Christmas. By the time he was fifteen, he had transformed himself into the family's resident gourmet chef. If his mother had dismissed rather than embraced his interest when it first surfaced, chances are it would be hard to get him fry an egg.

Whenever Possible, Allow Teens to Select the Household Jobs They Want to Do

Remember: You can't mandate cooperation. Instead, let your teen have a significant say in choosing how she contributes to the management of the home. By involving her in the decision-making process, she is much more likely to take personal "ownership" of tasks she has negotiated to get.

It's Okay to Expect Help with Less Desirable Chores

Though most tasks will lend themselves to self-selection by different family members, there will always be some chores no one particularly wants to do. These must be divided up fairly so that no one suffers a disproportionate share of the burden. One example in her own family, says Ford, was emptying the dishwasher each night. "I decided that this was one task that I needed my daughter to do for me, so I asked her to take it on," recalls Ford. "It was clearly a task that she hadn't picked for herself, and her reaction was somewhat predictable: She screamed and complained and whined and moaned." Eventually, however, she did agree to do it, but only begrudgingly. She'd slam the door, sigh frequently, and generally emit nasty vibes designed to make sure her mother knew how unhappy she was. The solution: The two talked the issue over at length, and the mother was able to eventually communicate why she needed her daughter to help her in this way. Eventually, the daughter shed her nasty vibes and agreed to perform the task without resentment out of respect for her mother. It wasn't long before the daughter found herself benefiting in two ways—first, she felt the genuine satisfaction of being responsible, and second, her mother's better mood and gratitude led to a spirit of reciprocation where she ended up doing favors for her daughter.

Bribes Do Work—Some of the Time

For special projects like cleaning out the garage or a big junky closet, Ford will either pay her daughter in cash or in *quid pro quos*—taking her, for example, to the local drug store to buy cosmetics. "For special jobs," says Ford, "I am totally *for* bribing because, when you think about it, that's how everybody works in this country." Payment is sometimes negotiated in advance based on what the daughter thinks the job is worth and what the mother can afford. Ford is also quick to point out that such payment is above and beyond her daughter's allowance, which is not tied to chores. "The reason I give her an allowance is so that she can learn how to manage money," says Ford, explaining the distinction. "She makes her regular contributions to the household because she lives here, and her reward for this is the satisfaction of contributing to our shared household."

Try a Trick from the B.F. Skinner Playbook

Sometimes the best rewards are the ones that come as a surprise. Once when his family household had been running particularly smoothly for several weeks, a father handed each of his twin teenagers a $20 bill. "What's this for?" the boys asked. Replied their father: "You guys have really been contributing to our home lately, and I just wanted to give you a token of my personal appreciation." As business managers and rat experimenters have long known, a surprise bonus like this can really be motivating, often much more so, in fact, than *predictable* rewards. After their intermittent reinforcement, the twin sons were all the more determined to keep up the good work at home.

Communication Is Key

If you do find yourself in a rancorous relationship with your teenager over chores, be willing to try different kinds of communication to untangle the discord. Here are some ways that parenting experts recommend you do this:

- Try to always remember that the worst situations can contain within them the best opportunities for improving your relationship.
- Look beneath the surface and really strive to see what the teen is trying to tell you with his or her refusal to do a given job.
- Remember that when it comes to communicating with a teen, some-

times less is more. Instead of launching a lengthy lecture, buy a pack of the *smallest* size Post-it™ Notes (the smaller the note, the less room for lecturing). Then write a short, positive, appreciative note and fasten it to your teen's door. Example: "Dear Bob, would you please empty the dishwasher by 9:30 tonight, and please don't bang it! Thanks a lot. Love, Dad." Ford has advocated this approach in the "Parenting with Love and Laughter" classes she teaches in Seattle, and the feedback from parents has been great.

- When you do need to have a face-to-face and heart-to-heart discussion with your teen, try to arrange to do this in a public place like a restaurant. That way, both teenager and parent alike are obligated to maintain a certain sense of decorum—that is, no screaming or door slamming.

- Be willing to negotiate. One stepmother, who wanted her son to do the dishes after dinner, approached the discussion this way: "I know I have a tendency to be the wicked stepmother sometimes, and I do have a quirk about getting the dishes done by 7:00 P.M. But I'm really wondering if you'd cooperate with me on this one—if you will, I will try to make it up to you in another way. Is there something you'd like from me?" Even if a teen doesn't have anything in particular in mind, says Ford, a parent who makes the effort to ask is both showing respect and giving the teen a sense of power, something most teens feel they lack.

- Don't be too quick to assume your own motives and desires are realistic. One mother realized she was being unreasonably autocratic when her teenage daughter and her partner both ganged up on her. "They asked me, 'What makes your way the right way? Maybe our way is the right way, too,'" the mother recalls. "I had to stop and ask myself if perhaps I was being unreasonable. Instead of getting locked into a power struggle, we explored the issue together and made some compromises."

- Finally, remember you're the parent and they're the teenagers, and there *will* be times you have to put your foot down. On such occasions, know clearly what it is you're hoping to achieve, and don't squander your legitimate parental power on trivialities. Don't, for instance, invoke your power for a wayward sock—save it for something truly important, like curfew or safety issues.

Family Meetings: The Secret to Successful Household Management

If running your household is truly to succeed as a cooperative venture, all family members must periodically regroup to analyze how things have been going—and participate in deciding what, if any, modifications must be made. In the eight-member Fumia household, family meetings are held every two or three weeks. The form these meetings take has been ritualized into two distinct parts—a pragmatic discussion of work expectations, followed by a clearing the air of each family member's feelings. Here's how they handle their sessions:

- Before each meeting, the parents post in prominent view an agenda that lists the topics of discussion. Each kid is free to add items to this agenda.

- The parents alternate roles—during one meeting, for instance, the mother will serve as the meeting's facilitator and the father will keep detailed notes. The next meeting, they switch.

- The children bring posters and markers to the meeting to update their upcoming roles in the chores rotation. Because of the size of their family, the Fumias assign two people to do the dishes each night. Regular chores, from cleaning to recycling, are also divided on an alternating schedule that assures everyone gets some practice at doing the different jobs.

- During the ensuing discussion, the family does group problem-solving for any areas of conflict. If a daughter is having trouble finding time to empty the dishwasher, for instance, the family tries to find a workable answer. "Maybe it turns out that Susie can do this job three days a week, Johnny can do it three days, and my husband or I will do it the other night," says Fumia. "Whatever the answer, we do try to give everyone a chance to have some input."

- It's critical that the parents themselves both do chores as well. "It's *very* problematic if one of the adults thinks they are a king or a queen who doesn't need to do any housework." When this happens, the kids get the idea that there is a kind of protected class absolved from membership in the household team. This also sends a message that chores are inherently onerous, something that you should try to avoid if you have the power to do so.

- The chores allocation also allows for some flexibility that takes into account each family member's circumstances. For example, when a given child enters high school, studying necessarily becomes a high priority. Or if a parent has to travel and work lots of overtime at her job, this gets factored in, too. College-bound teens and traveling parents alike are, of course, not relieved of *all* chores responsibility in the Fumia household. But they do earn a little slack. Those who provide this slack do so with the knowledge that they may one day ask for, and receive, reciprocation.

- By the end of the first half of the family meeting, everybody has made his or her own list enumerating his or her specific household responsibilities till the next meeting. Each child posts his or her list in their bedroom for easy reference.

- The second half of the meeting is devoted to venting feelings, which, if kept bottled up, might otherwise pollute the sense of cooperative team work that underlies their generally harmonious household management. The Fumias use a technique called *faith sharing* often employed in group counseling. Basically, this technique gives everyone a turn to say anything they want, and no one is allowed to respond, argue, or otherwise generate an instant comeback till much later. One teen, for instance, might say, "I am really sick and tired of everybody's congregating in my room all the time. I found an empty Coke can in my closet, and I know I didn't put it there. This really bugs me—I feel I need and am entitled to some privacy." Even as he's saying this, his siblings are chomping at the bit to argue the point, thinking to themselves that the only reason they even go in his room is because he's hogging the Nintendo machine for himself. But instead of verbalizing these responses immediately, they write down notes. Then the next family member has a chance to speak, and so forth, till everyone has gotten their peeves and complaints off their chests.

- Only afterward does the meeting facilitator go back and initiate a discussion about how to solve the problem. Example: One daughter had complained that getting her driver's license had only turned her into a twenty-four-hour-a-day chauffeur for the other kids. During the later discussion phase, she and her parents compromised in two ways. First, the daughter was free to say no to such requests if she was studying for a test or doing something else that was very important. And second, her parents agreed to limit her on-call time, as much as possible, to 3:00 to 5:00 P.M. The daughter understood and agreed that she might be asked to do some chauffeuring at other hours if it was really important. The bottom line was that they successfully worked out a compromise that all could live by.

The Wisdom of the Roadside

One final bit of advice for raising teens may seem a bit corny, but it can work. Consider posting the following little piece of Americana somewhere in prominent display in your house. These rules to live by may be most often found in the form of shellacked wooden plaques in roadside tourist gift shops. Tackiness of presentation, however, does not invalidate the essential wisdom of these dicta:

1. If you take it out, put it back.
2. If you open it, close it.
3. If you throw it down, pick it up.
4. If you take it down, hang it up.
5. If you wear it, hang it up.
6. If you eat out of it, wash it.
7. If you make a mess, clean it up.
8. If you turn it on, turn it off.
9. If you empty it, fill it.
10. If you lose it, find it yourself.
11. If you borrow it, put it back where it belongs.
12. If you move it, return it.
13. If it rings, answer it.
14. If it howls or meows, feed it or let it out.
15. If it cries, love it.

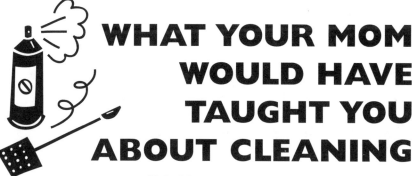

Chapter 7

WHAT YOUR MOM WOULD HAVE TAUGHT YOU ABOUT CLEANING

(If She Hadn't Just Done It for You While You Slept)

People who aren't clean or hygienic always say those things about clean people.

> —Israeli First Lady, Sara Netanyahu, responding to two ex-nannys who accused her of being pathologically clean

I am convinced that self-sufficiency in domestic areas is indispensable for day-to-day grounding and well-being. I have always said that a man cannot be truly happy unless he washes his own clothes. How else can one cleanse the soul? And why would any man ever think it reasonable for someone else to clean his sweat and filth? Should we not clean up our own messes?

> —George S.

There are times when I convince my husband to do work around the house knowing he'd rather be outside having fun. He gets very quiet and focused—and he cleans like a white tornado. I've been known to chase after him, and say, "Why don't you talk to me?" He'll say, "Get away from me. I'm getting it done as fast as possible."

> —Patricia M.

Priscilla's Story

"Whoever said 'Cleanliness is next to godliness' must have had a pretty unimaginative view of the divine, don't you think? And a nasty passive-aggressive streak, to want to make people feel guilty over dusty floors and tarnished silver and dog hair on the furniture.

"Anyway, I am that supposedly rarest of women, the slob. Please understand—as a person I'm as clean as the next gal, but I think it's possible to be a clean person in a less-than-sterile atmosphere. When Wallace comes around for a nuzzle, it's not as if he encounters an off smell. I am in the habit of bathing. But I don't notice housekeeping things.

"I will—so Wallace likes to tell people in scandalized tones—use a book for a coaster on a hot summer's day, so that a glass of iced tea sweats all over it! Or I'll slop milk over the edge of my bowl of cereal and not mop it up immediately, and it seeps into the crack in the center of the table and curdles in there! And the next day Wallace's nostrils will be flaring in a particular way, and later I'll catch him with the table pulled apart, swabbing with his anti-germ solvent.

"It isn't that I don't like a clean house. It's just that I find there are so many things I'd rather do than clean a house. My mother cleaned with a grudge hovering over her. It was a palpable cloud of resentment and servitude that she couldn't acknowledge because she wasn't even conscious of it. I won't be that way; I simply refuse.

"I find the current Martha Stewart craze to be particularly interesting. It's all about gracious living as conceived of by Martha—doing your own topiary, making cookies that look like miniature Renoirs or Raphaels (mine, when I do make some, tend to look like Pollocks), and so forth. I call her The Dominatrix of Gracious Living. But she never talks about the stuff you're asking about—the basics, the fundamentals, who scoops up the dog's mess in the yard. Well, she has a maid for that, no doubt. Raising her little hens and nibbling at her edible flowers, she reminds me of Marie Antoinette. It's not merely 'Let them eat cake'—now it's 'Let them eat exquisitely decorated cake.'

"Whenever I get on my Martha Stewart rant, certain people will leap up and say that I must be envious of her, that my so-called hostility is born of deep jealousy over her mastery of the womanly arts. This is non-sense. Besides, I do have the one thing which Martha lacks: a husband.

"My advice to women everywhere is to stop paying attention to Martha and start looking for a man like Wallace. He cleans with a joyful heart, or at least with a chipper one. He actually hums.

"Thanks to Wallace, we live in a very neat home, with the exception of one room, which is mine to defile as I please. Wallace is not allowed to neaten or dust it or clean it in any way. Every so often, perhaps every year or two, I do clean it. I get into a sort of frenzy, and I put away books alphabetically and throw out magazines and beat the rugs and scrape cobwebs out of the corners and rediscover lost coffee mugs with bizarre calcified oddments in them.

"And I must admit I find it tremendously satisfying—because I've *chosen* to do it, because nobody is forcing me to do it, and because I can really see a difference when I've finished.

"If you dust a room every week, you really can't see what you've accomplished, can you? I love a big, dramatic project. What I can't abide is maintenance."

Wallace's Story

"Aside from my very traditional childhood—Dad worked, Mom took care of the house—there were two events that shaped my attitude toward the subject of cleaning. The first came when I was working as a hospital orderly in college. I was around nineteen, and one of my first days on the job they sent me up to the OB/GYN floor. When I got there, the nurse in charge led me into a delivery room that had just been used and told me to clean it. There was no training or advice offered.

"If you haven't been in a delivery room lately, know this—birth is a *very* messy business. After standing there for what seemed like an hour trying to figure out where to even start, I started mopping and sopping, and eventually I had the whole place clean, rubbed down with alcohol, the whole bit. From this I learned that I could wade into a distasteful situation and reestablish some order.

"A few years later I was working as an office assistant for a famous research scientist (a woman—let's call her Dr. Clochard) who was married to a fire captain. She had to be away at a conference one night while her husband was scheduled to work, so she asked me if I would look after their two sons, ages ten and twelve, for the night. They lived in a big old house that supposedly was listed on some historical register—a really nice-looking place. I guess the historical inspectors hadn't checked the inside, though. When you walked in the door you got hit with a smell that was a cross between an ancient Egyptian tomb and a kennel.

"The kennel smell was explained by the fireman's two Dobermans which he kept in the basement. After proudly showing me the dogs, he locked them into their chamber and told me that under no circumstances was I to go near them, and not to let the kids near them, either. Then he was off to the firehouse until the morning.

"The kitchen was a total disaster—stacks and stacks of dishes, with cumulus clouds of mold that appeared to be growing as I watched. But it was in the bathroom where the real squalor lay. Apparently in the Clochard family it was customary to just throw things over your shoulder when you were finished with them. So the bathroom tile was a landscape of discarded toothpaste tubes, deodorant cans, shampoo bottles, soap wrappers, and so forth, which were interspersed with globs of toothpaste. The floor itself was coated with a thick furze of human hair and towel lint.

"The boys eventually went to bed and pretty soon so did I. Dr. Clochard had generously offered their bed, but when I stripped down to my skivvies and pulled back the comforter . . . The horror! The horror! So I spent the night in the den, sleeplessly huddling on a leather chair that seemed relatively clean, imagining that legions of cooties were scuttling across my skin, yearning passionately for my days of cleaning up hospital rooms. Beneath the floorboards I could hear the Dobermans growling.

"From this second formative experience I learned that you can reach a point of no return—that you can let the basic routines of civilized life get so out of whack that there is simply no getting caught up. What the Clochards demonstrated was not just eccentricity or the result of neglect caused by busy schedules. It was pathological. I couldn't imagine how a person could remain sane in that house.

"Did I mention that Dr. Clochard's field was behavioral psychology?

"Priscilla thinks I exaggerate when I tell this story, but I swear it's all true. She likes to think 'it couldn't happen here'—that even she, with her abysmal lack of housekeeping motivation, would never let things get so bad. Maybe not, but I'm not taking any chances."

Becoming Mr. Clean

Each year in the Midwest, several tons of topsoil erode from every acre of cropland. Until I became a homeowner, I always wondered where all that dirt went. Now I know.

A perennial housecleaning question is this: Should you dust or vacuum first? In my case, such a question is perhaps a bit premature. Better ask: Should you herbicide the living room or use a hoe on it first?

Of course, after eleven years of marriage and an equal number before that living on my own, it wasn't as if I'd developed no ideas about cleaning a house. Like a self-taught painter who works in the primitive style of a "naïf," I'd developed my own system for moving dirt around. Still, I'm the first to acknowledge that I am not a strong cleaner. At the old-dog-hoping-to-learn-new-tricks age of forty-three, I decided to do something about it.

If you want to get better at golf, tennis, or any other high-skill physical enterprise, I reasoned, there is only so much you can pick up on your own. To reach the next level, it's important to get a mentor.

For most guys, the cleaning mentor is their wife. Debbie, bless her heart, has tried to help remedy my cleaning inadequacies. But learning from her is a bit like having a spouse teach you how to drive a stick shift. The word *dunderhead*, for instance, stings less when coming from someone you don't share a bed with. And so I offer this chapter to all those squalor-challenged guys—and more than a few squalor-challenged women like Priscilla—who need some education in the finer points of the de-dirting arts.

When I told Debbie about my plan to pay a professional maid her hourly rate not to clean our house but to teach me how to clean it, she was all for it. After I let the idea set in for a while, I asked Debbie if she would mind my hiring one of those topless maids that you sometimes see advertised in the sports pages of the newspaper. She smirked and suggested I hire instead a sixty-one-year-old friend of hers named Margaret Valenzi.

Margaret, a former Austrian and all-around wonderful woman, learned how to clean at her mother's knee. Since then, she's worked as a domestic for much of her life—in fact, her early years sound like a chapter out of Dickens. Here's what she told me when I called her up to hire her as my professor:

Shortly after World War II, when she was thirteen, Margaret's family immigrated to the United States. The war had left them virtually destitute, so her father took two jobs and worked sixteen hour days, six days a week. But even this could barely keep the family afloat. When he saw an ad in the local paper for a live-in maid, he volunteered Margaret for the job—only to be told by the lady of the house that Margaret was too young. Undaunted, he placed his own ad in the paper, and a week later received a call from the same woman who had earlier turned him down. This time, he told her Margaret was sixteen. She was hired on the spot.

For the next five years, Margaret lived on the palatial estate of a department store magnate and his extremely demanding wife. She was paid $3.50 a week to start—a salary that grew to $13 a week after five years.

Not that low pay translated into low demands. She had to work extremely hard for her employer, Mrs. X, who apparently considered cleanliness not next to but quite a bit above godliness. "Her standards," recalls Margaret, "were so high it was almost like a disease." The first time Margaret cleaned the kitchen floor, for instance, she made the mistake of using a mop—a not altogether unheard of tool for the job. Mrs. X, who literally wore white gloves during her cleaning inspections, told Margaret that simply would not do—and made her rescrub every square inch of the floor on her hands and knees.

Another time, Mrs. X discovered a single bread crumb that had somehow eluded Margaret's eye. "What are you doing here?" she snapped at the young girl. "Trying to grow potatoes?"

During her younger years, Margaret was too cowed to talk back to her taskmaster, though she would occasionally burst into tears. But as she grew into womanhood, Margaret began to stand up for herself—and when the demands for perfection became too abusive, she would simply walk out of the house. "Then 'Mrs. X' would call and beg me to come back," she says.

Given such a background, it's a wonder that Margaret doesn't hate cleaning today. But as I would learn during my four-hour lesson, she approaches the tasks with a skillfulness and dignity that I could not help but admire. Like many people whose expertise exists in areas that are not afforded much respect by our society, Margaret tended to shrug off her considerable household skills as "nothing special." But to me, her work was inspiring.

Equally interesting, I found, was that Margaret had not internalized the lunatic standards of her boss. She does a great job cleaning, but clearly understands that there is a line between clean and *clean*—and her experiences over the years have taught her that hunting down and eradicating the last mote of dust is no way to live. "I do have sympathy for men whose wives treat them the way my employer treated me," she says. "My advice is to just let it go when cleaning becomes irrational. Total spotlessness, when it gets down to it, is so unimportant in life."

Hands-On Learning

Total spotlessness, to be sure, is not a problem that afflicts our household. In the interest of learning, I asked Debbie if we could "let things go" for a week or two so that when Margaret came over for my lesson, I'd have lots to practice on. Debbie, who I may have mentioned earlier is a "let it go" spouse by nature anyway, didn't have any problem with this.

Two weeks later, our house was a complete mess: toys spilled everywhere, dirty dishes piled up in the sink, mud prints dappling the kitchen floor, a menagerie of dust bunnies and even larger dust fauna, a toilet that is, frankly, disgusting.

To add some motivating fuel to my lesson, I had scheduled Margaret to come the day before friends were traveling a thousand miles to visit us. This was the only part of my plan that made Debbie nervous—like many women and some men, her standards of neatness and cleanliness skyrocket when guests are coming. It seems to be deeply ingrained in her synapses that a dirty house reflects very poorly on her—a kind of my home, myself psychic equation.

I am really trying to capture some of this panic myself. Our friends, Tim and Susan, are bringing their ten-month-old twins—little crawlers with the urge to mouth any suitably sized items in their environment. What if Tim and Susan look under the bed and see seeds sprouting in the dust bunnies? I ask myself rhetorically. Or what if they announce after looking at our kitchen, "I'm sorry, but we simply can't eat in this home—*it's not safe.*"

Try as I might to conjure such humiliating scenes, I can't quite talk myself into believing any of them. *So what if the house is less than operating-room antiseptic?* I find myself thinking. One of my aunts, a borderline obsessive-compulsive who often tried to enlist me in her cleaning rituals, paradoxically used to say, "Oh well, you eat a peck of dirt before you die."

Yeah, I say, a peck of dirt. It builds up immunity—those cute little twins will leave our house healthier than ever!

I know this won't play, of course, even as I acknowledge that I lack a cleaning impulse turbocharged with deep-seated notions of self-worth. Call me a dirt sociopath, but I know that doing a good job is unlikely to be rewarded by the cessation of an anxiety I don't feel.

But just because I can't summon my wife's motivation to do this job right, it doesn't mean I can't find a great reason to act. And this reason isn't even particularly hard to find: *I love my wife.* My taking responsibility for this job will make her happy—more so than buying her flowers or surprising her with a love letter and chocolate cookie or any of the other little gestures I have occasionally provided. Though you'll never learn this from a love song, cleaning a toilet, I suspect, may just be the best way of all to say I love you.

Let the Lessons Begin

Margaret arrived at noon on Friday. "The place to start," she told me, "is getting the right supplies." In her right hand, she holds a basket loaded with vinegar, a glass cleaner, a liquid cleanser for use on sinks and the bath tub, a non-abrasive cleanser for use on stainless steel, a general purpose oil soap for use on most other surfaces, a disinfectant, and a furniture polish. In her other hand, she held a bag of rags—wash towels, torn T-shirts, and scraps of old flannel bed sheets for cleaning windows and glass. "When we're done with these rags," she said, "we just throw them in the wash—it gets too expensive not to reuse them over and over."

After familiarizing myself with the different cleaning products, I asked Margaret where I should start.

"You start in the kitchen," she said. "The kitchen is my worst enemy, so I get that out of the way first."

"What about the bathroom?" I asked, mentally flashing on the furry poultice that had grown up around the toilet. "Is that the second worst enemy?"

"Sure," said Margaret. "We'll do that next—once you have those two areas done, the rest is a breeze."

During the next half hour, Margaret brought an efficiency expert's skill to the job at hand. Here, in summary form, is what she showed me how to do:

1. Make It Fun

When she cleans her own home, Margaret told me, she puts on some music first. Though I can't do this today—I am, after all, interviewing Margaret as we move along—I made a mental note to put on my old *Singing Nun* album the next time I clean. "What about a beer?" I ask Margaret. "Sure," she says. "Sometimes I'll have a glass of wine while I clean. Just don't drink too much." Mental note #2: In the future, reserve cleaning for Miller time.

2. De-Clutter Everything

Cleaning around a mess is a major pain, so Margaret instructed me to put everything away—groceries in the appropriate cabinets, the kids' toys, school papers, and art work in newly designated cubby holes, cans and empty jars in their recycling bins, and so on. "Wherever it goes," she said with an almost Zen-like simplicity, "that's where it goes." As I was trying to figure out just where certain items of detritus go, Margaret nodded at the trash can. Be ruthless, she said. Throw out junk you don't like, or take it to Goodwill. People who save stuff because they think they'll need it someday almost never need it—and if they do, they can't find it anyway, because the house is just too cluttered.

3. Start the Dishes

We had a good week's supply of cutlery, glasses, and flatware that had gradually covered all our countertops. Margaret told me to rinse all the food off the plates then fill one side of the sink with hot, soapy water and let the dishes soak therein while we cleaned the rest of the kitchen. When the last dish was in the soap stew, I surveyed the progress. Countertops once invisible with clutter were now beautifully, marvelously clear and full of promise. What's more, the kitchen had been evacuated of four loads of trash. It was like being suddenly cured of a kind of domestic constipation. I felt a jolt of genuine satisfaction—the first of what would prove to be numerous spurts of housecleaning endorphins. In fact, I was so impressed by the progress that it occurred to me I'd done enough here—time to move on to the second enemy.

4. Work from Top to Bottom

Margaret, who still has traces of her Austrian accent, chuckled Germanically at my suggestion to move on. "We haven't started to clean yet," she said. Though I suspect she was thinking of adding *you dunderhead*, she kept it to herself. At this point, she filled a bucket halfway with hot water and added enough oil soap to get some suds. She immersed a rag in the water, then squeezed most of the water out of it. Starting with the door ledges, we went around the kitchen, wiping off all horizontal surfaces. Every minute or so, she told me to ring out the rag and moisten it slightly with new soapy water. It's amazing how much grunge had been lurking unnoticed in our kitchen. In fact, in some spots—especially the top of the refrigerator, the dust was so thick that the moistened rag only made it pill up into grotesque snake-like rolls of blackened filth.

"When it gets this bad," said Margaret, "you're better off using the sweeper first." I vacuumed the top of our fridge, then used the moistened rag to make it spotless. But we're not done with the ice box yet—Margaret next had me roll it out from the wall and vacuum up the squalor hiding behind. Finally, she instructed me to open the door and remove the meat tray. A previously unseen substance that is perhaps best described as bloody gelatin covered the refrigerator floor. I de-gunked and washed it thoroughly. For my efforts, I was rewarded with another jolt of cleaning endorphins.

5. Wash the Windows

In one hand, Margaret held a moistened piece of flannel bed sheet, and in the other, a dry cloth. She showed me how to keep the cleaning motion unidirectional—up and down on the glass—as opposed to circular. This helps prevent streaking. She also dried the windows with her opposite hand, again to eliminate streaking. Though my attempts to mimic the technique are not entirely streak-free, I was slowly getting the hang of it.

6. Go Where No Man Has Gone Before

In the course of our work, I happened to ask Margaret how often she cleans her microwave. "Everyday," she said. She noticed my look of surprise and added, "We better take a look." Inside the microwave, bits of spillover food had virtually alloyed themselves to the bottom. When my scrubbing efforts failed to eliminate the stains, Margaret gently reminded me that I needed to "use muscle." It was around this time that I discovered that I had begun to perspire. When I finally finished, Margaret says, "We better look at the back of the microwave—ah, look at this." The vents on the back had never been cleaned in the nine years we had owned this apparatus. It's a wonder the thing works at all. Under Margaret's watchful eye, I vacuumed out dust that predates our children. Afterward, we checked behind all the appliances for treasure troves of squalor. We were not disappointed. The hungry vacuum cleaner was not soon sated.

7. Preventive Maintenance

"You know, Jim, if you do a little bit everyday," Margaret told me, "your kitchen won't ever get this bad." Particularly important, she added, is to wipe down the inside of the microwave every time we use it. She also suggested we buy decent floor mats to put by the doors inside and out—that way, we can stop a lot of dirt and dust from invading the house. We do have a small throw rug in the kitchen, which Margaret takes outside to shake. I have occasionally shaken this same rug, which usually results in sand in my eyes and mouth. Watching Margaret, I learned the proper technique—turn your head to the side, close your eyes, and give it two fierce snapping shakes of the sort used by rat terriers in their own work.

8. Vacuum and Mop Floors

At this point in the cleaning, I was definitely starting to feel exercised. I checked my pulse and was pleased to discover that I was approaching the target zone for aerobic benefits. The kitchen floor was encrusted here and there with spilled oatmeal and yogurt, and each nook and cranny yielded what might be described as accidental trail mix—peanuts, cereal flakes, raisins, the occasional desiccated pea. Mental note: Find out if any scavengers make good pet animals. Margaret suggested that I vacuum the floor, then showed me how to use the squeeze mop to finish the job. It's important to rinse out the mop frequently and to dry as you go along to prevent streaks. Moving along one square yard at a time, I made quick work of the floor, which soon looked better than it has since we moved in. "Doesn't that look better?" asked Margaret. "Don't you *feel* better?" Yes, I had to admit. Yes!

9. Finish Dishes and Clean the Sink

After I wipe down the counters, Margaret instructed me to wash the dishes by hand and rinse them in hot water—the hotter the rinse water, she explained, the more quickly they'll dry. I did this, then used a liquid cleaner on our stainless steel sink and the softer abrasive on the faucet. As Margaret exhorted me once again to "use muscle," the sink began to shine. At last I have finished off the worst enemy, and I found myself bathed in the glow of my accomplishment. "Usually," said Margaret, "I take a break now, have a cup of coffee and just enjoy how clean things look." It sounded tempting, but I didn't want to lose momentum. The cunning toilet awaited upstairs—I wanted to attack the next worst enemy now, before I lost my nerve.

10. Onward Cleaning Soldiers, Marching As to War!

Over the course of the next two hours, Margaret showed me the tricks of the housecleaning trade. Many of the same principles I learned in the kitchen—that is, declutter, work from top to bottom, and so on—apply to most rooms. In the bathroom, she instructed me to work from tub to sink to toilet, which is the order of least to most likely to be infested with germs. Once the toilet has been cleaned and disinfected, she said, throw those rags into the laundry bag—don't reuse them elsewhere in the house. This is the one point where I think Margaret may have underestimated my household common sense. Even I could figure out that you don't employ used toilet cleaning rags to, say, swab out the family Crock-Pot.

11. Beyond the Bathroom: Furniture and Bedrooms

The rest of the house was, as promised, a breeze. To tackle the dust bunnies under the beds and other hard-to-access spots, Margaret suggested I use a dust mop sprayed with a dust cleaner. I had to ask Debbie if we have a dust mop, and when the answer was yes, I followed up with, "Where is it?" For more easily accessible surfaces, Margaret is a big fan of the vacuum sweeper, and she showed me how to use it not just on the floors, but on the floorboards and windowsills as well. She then attached a circular brush to the end of the vacuum and demonstrated how to clean the living room chairs and couch. When I removed the couch pillows to get underneath, I found an assortment of coins, Lego pieces, tiny dinosaurs, and what looked to be enough sand to fill a small sandbox. (Later, when I mentioned this sand to Debbie and expressed the need for our kids to wipe their feet at the door, she quickly nipped my budding smugness. "That's not sand," she said. "That's salt from the pretzels you eat when you're watching TV.")

12. Make It Glow

Our house has loads of wood furniture, and the final step was to polish these items to a high gloss. Margaret instructed me to spray furniture polish on a piece of folded flannel bed sheet—don't spray directly on the wood. Then moving in a unidirectional manner, she buffed the wood before using a dry flannel sheet to buff it further. About five hours after we started, the house was at last clean—with the sole exceptions, that is, of the basement and the rooms on the third floor where Debbie and I keep our home offices. "The first time takes the longest," summed up Margaret. "After that, you can cut corners and the job will be just as well done. Remember, it is much easier to clean than it is to describe in words *how* to clean. Do it next time by yourself, and then you'll have it—you won't have to think about it, you'll just know what to do."

Open Your Eyes

Margaret, to be sure, is the first to admit that her system is not the only way to clean. The important thing, she says, is to find a routine that works for you, one that allows you to clean your house in as short a time as possible to the standards you and your mate both agree make sense.

For me, hiring Margaret as a cleaning teacher was a tremendous eye-opener. Though the description of my lesson is condensed, I needed to ask her myriad dumb questions, from how to wash dishes (wash rag and elbow grease) to what to do with the dirty bucket water (toss it outside or down the laundry room drain). Her wealth of knowledge was astonishing.

In the process, I learned firsthand how difficult cleaning an entire house is, how physically exhausted it can make you—but also how satisfying it can be to complete the job right. Even for those couples who are happily traditional in their division of labor, I can't recommend this exercise strongly enough. Old-style, sole breadwinning men: If you've never cleaned your whole house before, try it at least once. You will come to value your mate's contributions more than you can now imagine. And this newfound appreciation will almost certainly strengthen your marriage.

As for the rest of us, learning to do this job well will give you a giant leap on the road to household fairness—and all the benefits this bestows upon a relationship.

For apprentice and seasoned cleaners alike, the following tip sheet may help you make quicker work of housecleaning. The sources for some of these nuggets of insight are Don Slifer, marketing manager for the national Merry Maids residential home cleaning company, which cleans over 200,000 homes per month, and Don Aslett, owner of Varsity Contractors cleaning service and author of a host of best-selling books on cleaning, including *Is There Life After Housework?* and *Clutter's Last Stand.*

These guys *know* cleaning—Merry Maids, for instance, generated sales of $150 million in 1995, and Don Aslett has made enough money from his cleaning business, that he can afford to spend winters at his second home in Hawaii.

Don't feel you have to incorporate all of these suggestions at once— just add one or two each time you clean, and you may find you're doing a better job faster as time goes by. Who knows? Maybe you'll get good enough that one day you, too, can clean a hideaway house in the South Seas.

How to Stop the Dirt Invasion

- Much as it may seem that dust spontaneously erupts out of nowhere, most of it gains entry into your home from the larger world. On the outside of every entryway, place a mat of artificial grass for foot wiping.

- Post a *Please Wipe Your Feet* sign by the mat—and supplement this with voice commands whenever necessary.

- On the inside of entryways, place a commercial-grade floor mat to snag whatever dirt has eluded capture outside. Call the Yellow Pages for a janitorial supply company in your area.

- During winter months, remove shoes and boots as soon as you enter your house—and insist your kids do likewise.

- Frequently replace your furnace and air-conditioning filters, and make sure windows are caulked properly.

Reduce the Need to Clean

- Clear out the clutter—your's and your children's. When your kids outgrow their toys, consider giving them to a local day-care center. There's still a lot of fun left in them. Ditto with books.

- Pigeonhole the stuff you do need to keep. Go to an office supply superstore and get filing cabinets to store everything from product instructions and warranties to tax records.

- Purchase office trays for school clutter—flyers, homework, artwork, and so on.

- Design your environment to stay clean. For example, avoid baroque flourishes where dust can accumulate. And remember that dark colors show dirt more than light or medium colors—so paint and upholster accordingly.

- Practice prevention a little each day. Steam, for instance, loosens dirt—so keep an old towel by the shower and dry the shower walls before you dry yourself.

- Don't clean what's not dirty. This advice sounds straightforward enough, but I have an aunt who periodically washes her already immaculate walls—the only dirt on them is the residue from the water and soap used to clean them.

- If you or someone you love is truly obsessed with cleaning, contact a therapist. It may be that your synapses, not your sinks, are contaminated. All joking aside, for people who truly suffer from

Obsessive-Compulsive Disorder (OCD), cleaning can become a full-time preoccupation that can destroy families and, in a very real way, ruin lives. Advances in medications and behavioral therapies can often bring relief to those who know their cleaning throttles have somehow become stuck open.

Get the Right Tools

- Aslett recommends that you need only four professional cleaning solutions, which can be purchased at your local janitorial supply store: a disinfectant, a heavy-duty degreaser, a glass cleaner, and a neutral all-purpose cleaner like Murphy's Oil Soap.

- Watch for sales and buy in bulk for greater savings.

- You can also buy well-designed, durable tools from a janitorial supply company—commercial grade brooms, sponges, squeegees, and so on.

- Buy top-rated power equipment—a good vacuum cleaner, for instance, may cost you a little more initially, but it will save you tons of a commodity more valuable than money—your time.

- Keep a hand vac on hand for small spills, crumbs, and cobwebs.

- Always keep a bottle of seltzer water on hand for stains—use this to gently blot the affected area before the stain has a chance to set.

- Cloth diapers and cotton underwear make excellent, reusable cleaning rags.

- Lemon oil inside your shower can help repel hard-water deposits and accumulating soap scum.

- Designate a handy spot for your cleaning equipment and supplies—the easier these are to reach, the more likely someone will reach for them. Some families even keep a bucket of cleaning supplies and tools on each floor for maximum convenience.

Attack Strategies

- Do any outside chores in the early fall before the weather turns cold. Because you are going to be effectively sealed up in your home during winter months, fall cleaning is really more important than spring cleaning.

- Take care of messes when they first happen, that is, before spills have had a chance to congeal or be ground into microscopic pumice.

- To eliminate crayon marks, try concentrated dishwashing soap.

- Spray your dust mop with furniture polish for an easy way to dust floors and hard-to-reach woodwork.

- Consider using a squeegee to wash windows—use two drops of dishwashing detergent per gallon of water.

- Another good way to wash windows is to use inexpensive "non-shedding" paper towels and car windshield wiper fluid. Definitely make sure, however, that this stays out of reach of small children.

- Cleaning is a bit like eating—better to do a little each day while it's manageable rather than waiting till you're desperate and bingeing.

- Make every trip count—it's amazing how many trips up and down the stairs can be eliminated by a little strategic planning.

- Try to multiprocess to make cleaning more enjoyable—fold laundry, for instance, while watching a favorite TV show.

- Conversely, don't let yourself get distracted from the task at hand—don't answer the phone while cleaning, let your answering machine take messages.

- Avoid injuring yourself—use your legs to lift, not your back. And don't attempt to clean light bulbs with a wet cloth.

- For very difficult or dangerous jobs, such as mucking out third floor gutters, consider farming the job out to a professional. Even the most diehard do-it-yourselfers tend to balk at chimney sweeping.

- If you don't know how to do a chore—such as sorting the laundry properly or how to dust—don't try to wing it. Solicit the advice of a housemate or—even better—a local pro to show you how to do the job right. Chances are you'll learn skills that will let you clean better—and faster—than you can now imagine.

- To learn more about housecleaning from veterans, check out any of Don Aslett's books (to order, write to Cleaning Center, P.O. Box 39, Pocatello, ID 83204). *All-New Hints from Heloise: A Household Guide for the '90s* and *Mary Ellen's Complete Home Reference Book,* by Mary Ellen Pinkham, are also good.

- Practice, practice, practice! Cleaning is like golf—you do get better at it over time.

A Few Tips on Laundry

- Buy easy-to-care-for clothes—preshrunk, permanent press, plus any other adjective that translates into idiot proof indestructibility. Gross as this may sound to fashion purists, a robotics scientist I once interviewed swore by his all-polyester wardrobe.

- Sorting is one of the most time-consuming aspects of the laundering process. Consider buying four bins and label them White, Dark, Colors, and Delicates. Ask your family members to toss dirty clothes in the appropriate bin.

- Don't make a fetish out of folding. Underwear, gym socks, and most T-shirts, for instance, are not going to be ruined if you simply cram them into the drawer.

- If, like me, you aren't exactly sure which setting to use for the clothes washer and the dryer, have your family's master launderer draw the dials and indicate via arrows which settings to use for which kinds of clothes. Do this on Post-it™ Notes and affix them to the pertinent machine.

Chapter 8

OVERCOMING AN EDIBLE COMPLEX
Nutritious Meals Made Simple

Food is an important part of a balanced diet.
—Fran Liebowitz

If you can't stand the heat, get out of the kitchen.
—Harry Truman

When my brother's girlfriend, now wife, first stayed at his house, she complained vehemently that he had no eggs in his house—how could he let this happen? He said it had just become too much. Every time he moved he had to buy new eggs.
—Joe V.

My mother doled out non-regular chores as punishment. Roughing up a younger brother could draw you hours of having to help mom in the kitchen. Getting caught smoking could leave you setting the table and cleaning dishes for a week. After being drafted into the army, this was reinforced with KP (kitchen police), being given as the worst punishment short of incarceration. And it was. Other than eating, the kitchen was a dungeon, a place to serve a penance. To this day, I believe that people who say they enjoy their hours spent in the kitchen just don't get out enough.
—Joe V.

Lee's (Short) Story

"I am a writer with a specialty in food, health, and nutrition. Despite my interest in food, I'm like a lot of overworked Americans—I *don't* do a lot of everyday cooking. My best recipe is the fresh prepared food section of an upscale supermarket!

"Ask who cooked dinner in our house last night and the answer is, 'Do you mean the person who bought the home replacement meal (as they are called in the grocery trade) or the person who pressed the microwave buttons?' "

Brian's Story

"When I got my first apartment in college, sharing it with three other blockheads with even less cooking sense than I, my Mom made me a typed, spiral-bound cookbook with some favorite recipes. I used it for years and still open it every now and then (usually at Christmas to find a cookie recipe).

"She included a lot of recipes from an Erma Bombeck cookbook—an example being 'Stay in Bed Stew,' which called for cut-up stew meat, a can of cream of mushroom soup (what else?), and a cup of red "cooking wine" (that is, the stuff with salt in it, since I guess she assumed we wouldn't have any other kind of wine around).

"You glopped it all together, put it in the oven, then went to bed for about four hours.

"'Skid-Row Stroganoff' was another one—it called for hamburger, cream of mushroom soup, and—the height of elegance—sour cream, which somehow made food ethnic.

"Nowadays, sometimes it seems that my own little stressed-out family eats only whatever is in those plastic microwaveable boxes in the freezer. How do leftovers get in there if we never cook anything from scratch? This is a mystery.

"Actually, we do eat a lot of pasta that I cook for us—it's so easy and fast, and leftovers microwave fast, and my son Colin, who hates food on principle, will eat virtually nothing but.

"I've recently also gotten into making some plain lentils—just boiling some soaked lentils for about fifteen to twenty minutes, then having them around (in the fridge) to add to a sauce for pasta or polenta or rice. Lots of protein. Cheap. Easy. No meat. No fat.

"A couple times a month, I'll cook us a real, full-course, sit-down-at-the-table kind of meal that most of us got nightly when we were growing up in Ozzie-and-Harriet households. I don't mind doing this cooking when I have the time—it's fun for me, almost like a hobby.

"I think a lot of guys find cooking inside the house a little intimidating. Barbecuing on the grill seems somehow more what we evolved to do: fire and meat. But I say to my fellow cooking blockheads: Come inside the kitchen and broaden your horizons from the stone-age scenario.

"Men who know how to cook, by the way, are not exactly rare. Find a buddy with some culinary expertise, take a six-pack over to his house as a tuition payment, and ask him to teach you how to cook something good, healthy, and simple.

"Who knows? If you master Skid-Row Stroganoff today, tomorrow you might be ready to tackle Skid-Row Chicken Liver Mousseline with Pistachios finished off with a nice Skid-Row Chocolate Raspberry Dobostorte (neither of which, I might add, requires mushroom soup)."

Hunting, Gathering, Cooking

It's 6:00 P.M. and you just got home from work. Your kids are whining from hunger, you're starved yourself, and there's nothing to eat. Thus begins the mad, last minute scramble to prepare (or order by phone) the prepackaged fast-food biomass that is the today's stopgap substitute for yesteryear's homemade cuisine.

There's nothing wrong, of course, about ordering an occasional pizza. But if your family's "four basic food groups" have devolved into Pepperoni, Cheese, Crust, and Coke, you know in your heart that it's time to widen your culinary horizons.

Men, if you're like me, you may already cook "a little." Perhaps, like Brian, you cooked for yourself during your bachelor years and even enjoyed it a little. But once entering a relationship with your beloved, you have gradually abdicated all the cooking duties, save an occasional barbecue grilling. And on those evenings when you're cranky from hunger and the mewling of your progeny, who do you secretly blame for the lack of food on the table? Yourself?

Don't be absurd. Mom always had dinner ready—a four-courser at that. In that dark, sexist lobe of your brain, you blame your wife (and perhaps she blames herself, too) for failing to live up to the meat loaf extraordinaire standards both your mothers consistently met.

Maybe if you just roll your eyes back far enough, complain about potential heart problems you're developing from the McDonald's-and-Häagen-Dazs diet you've been on for months, and have patience, maybe, someday, your wife will see the light and transform herself into your mother.

This metamorphosis isn't likely to happen.

With a little advanced planning, both of you can provide your family with good, nutritious, *easy* meals—and save money in the process. The key, however, is being prepared ahead of time.

Planning and Shopping

One of the main problems with waiting until you're starved to cook is that you're too hungry then to make rational decisions. For many people, cooking *per se* is not all that daunting—it's trying to figure out *what* to cook at the last minute.

To help remedy this problem, Debbie and I sit down together every Sunday night and decide what meals we want to cook during the coming week. In our case, this is done quite informally—"Let's have chicken a couple times, pasta a couple times, and maybe burgers and grilled vegetables on Saturday."

Other people do a much more detailed planning process—and they reap the rewards of a week's worth of much more varied meals. Explains one California executive, "I prepare a detailed menu list each week, which takes about a half-hour of scouring my cookbooks for variety. If I know one of us has a meeting scheduled, I plan on cooking pasta that night because it's easy to fix, and you can heat it up if someone's running late. I tend to save the more complex cuisine for the weekends, when I have the time to indulge my passion for cooking. Once I have figured out the week's recipes, I make the grocery list.

"You can't believe how many of my friends, male and female alike, express astonishment at my doing this. But it really saves time and aggravation in the long run. You end up making only one trip a week to the grocery store, for instance. And you never have to endure that awful situation when you're surrounded by a starving family, have no idea what to cook, and your cupboard is so bare you couldn't cook even if you did have a meal in mind. Even with two kids, we never have to resort to fast-food restaurants."

If you're into computers, you can spend a few hours creating a weekly customized shopping list, complete with staples and specific ingredients that are called for in any upcoming recipes. Says Mike Finley, a computer consultant who has taken charge of shopping and cooking for his family, "I have the entire household supply and purchasing function on the PC, one benefit of which is that I can order different staples in bulk from the lowest-priced direct source. Each week, I print out individualized calendars that include such things as what days we'll be too busy to cook and must order out, what days we're expecting company, and what days any of us have to be somewhere else at dinner time."

I, too, am a big believer in the computerized shopping list. I print out a list of all the foods we regularly need, complete with an annotation that tells me in which aisle each can be found at in our local supermarket. (The one thing I *hate* about food shopping is the scavenger-hunt quality for uncommon items. For example, my wife asked me to get some couscous for her one week, and when I asked a stock boy where it was, he laughed and said, "What kind of animal is that?" Ten minutes later, we finally found it—it took longer to locate than to cook!) Based on our informal meal-planning, Debbie then goes through the list and checks all the items we'll need in the coming week. She also writes a *C* next to any item for which we have a coupon.

You don't have to have a computer, of course, to come up with such a sheet. Just write a one-time master list of everything you're likely to need, include a space for miscellaneous just in case, then photocopy a bunch of copies to use on successive weeks.

Armed with my own idiot-proof instruction sheet, I hop into the car with our kids and go shopping. Our local discount grocery store has come up with a great idea that I hope will spread quickly around the country: a supervised playroom for kids while their parent shops in peace. The playroom is equipped with toys, art supplies, Legos, and several interactive computer games. My kids love it.

The Five-Level Meal Plan

Assuming that your larder is now filled with the staples and foodstuffs that your family likes, it's time to get down to the business of putting food on the table. A plan that we have found extremely useful in my house is the Five-Level Meal Plan, which ranges from the extremely easy (Level One) to the dauntingly difficult (Level Five). Here's how it works:

Level One

This is a list of take-out and delivery food services in our area, everything from the kids' favorite pizza place and sub shops to the local delicatessen and restaurants that will deliver. On a piece of paper posted by the telephone, we have scribbled down the phone numbers (and, when applicable, fax numbers) for a half-dozen such places. We also have tacked up on the bulletin board the take-out menus from whichever of these places has them.

When we are all starved but too exhausted to think, let alone cook, we allow ourselves to resort to Level One. It's not particularly economical, so we don't make too regular a habit of it. We also try to make sure we vary things a bit—that is, pizza one night, then Chinese the next time we need to resort to Level One.

Level Two

These are nutritious, microwaveable convenience foods that take almost less time to make than dialing for take-out.

Every family, to be sure, is likely to have its own range of preferences for these kinds of foods. One woman who reviews the ever-expanding smorgasbord of available offerings is syndicated columnist Carolyn Wyman, a self-described junk food addict. Her column, cowritten with registered dietitian, Bonnie LeBlang, is called "Supermarket Sampler"— it appears in dozens of newspapers across the country.

Since Wyman eats such food, well, *professionally*, I asked her to tell me her personal favorites. "In the modern world of supermarkets and restaurant take-out, non-cooks can survive and even thrive," she told me, "but only if they are excellent shoppers. At least that's been my experience. Dinner can be as easy as knowing what are the best TV dinners—and loading up the freezer when they're on sale."

Wyman's picks include:

- Most Budget Gourmet entrees, including French Recipe Chicken, Penne Pasta, Mandarin Chicken, Chinese Style Vegetables and Chicken, and Gourmet Chicken Oriental Style;
- Most Stouffer's Lean Cuisines, especially Fiesta Chicken, Cafe Classics Bow-Tie Pasta and Chicken, and Three Bean Chili;
- Stouffer's Red Box Chicken Pie, Lasagna, Chicken a la King, and Bianco Pizza. Note: Stouffer's sells its delicious lasagna in a big, family size tray, says Wyman. Buy, heat, and serve it with a salad. Incidentally, the discount club stores like Costco and Price Club can be a great source of premium-quality, family-sized frozen meals at reasonable prices.

I personally like Healthy Choice's clam chowder and low-fat ice creams. You might want to experiment a little to find items each family member especially enjoys, then add these to your master shopping list. Keep an eye out for sales and coupons, and keep plenty on hand for Level Two Emergencies.

The problem with eating Level Two–style too often is that it's not much cheaper than eating take-out. "Unless we're talking sixty-nine cent, on-sale Michelina's or Yu Sings," sums up Wyman, "buying individual TV dinners for every member of a family or every guest can get expensive. Also, some guests might not realize that Stouffer's cooks a lot better than you and so be insulted."

Which brings us to . . .

Level Three

These are no-brainer foods that are nevertheless nutritious and extremely easy to make. On the bottom rung of Level Three are things like omelets, sandwiches, and canned or dried soup mixes. Your supermarket also offers plenty of by-the-kit type foods, says Wyman, that are good-tasting, cheap, easy-to-prepare things you can buy and build your meal around. A few of her recommendations:

- Buy one of those taco meal kits (containing tortillas, seasoning, and sauce), add some shredded cheese, lettuce, tomatoes, and ground beef, and set up a home taco bar. To make this even healthier, instead of using hamburger, substitute Green Giant's new Harvest Burgers or Recipes frozen vegetable crumbles. Most people won't notice the difference. Because people make their own tacos, it's less work for the chef, but most diners will think it's fun. Add beer and you have an adult party.

- Add ground beef or Green Giant Harvest Burger product to a can of kidney beans and another of canned or jarred chili-tomato mix (Del Monte, Hunt's, and Tabasco all make them) and—voila!—chili. Serve with supermarket bakery corn muffins and, for the adults, a good-quality beer.

- Buy a Boboli style pizza crust and add shredded cheese and your favorite toppings. Serve with a simple salad (you can even buy these precut and prepackaged by companies like Dole and Fresh Express). Fans of sweet Chicago-style pizza might want to try thawing frozen bread dough and spreading it in a pan as a substitute for Boboli.

- Stock up on your favorite jarred pasta sauces when they go on sale. Serve on spaghetti with a salad. Time invested: less than 15 minutes.

- Pick up a rotisserie chicken or two from your supermarket deli. Since the advent of Boston Market and Kenny Roger's, supermarket rotisserie chickens have gotten much better. They're also lots cheaper than their restaurant competitors, and so are the accompanying deli cole slaw and potato side dishes (I recommend the microwaveable and delicious Ore Ida Frozen Mashed Potatoes) that you can pick up while you're there.

- Cruise the gourmet or produce aisles for jarred or bottled Indian curry, Thai peanut, or other Oriental sauces (Hormel's House of Tang is one easily available brand of Oriental sauces). They can be a little pricey but will last through many meals. You can make a delicious pasta salad by combining some Thai peanut sauce with a little bit of cooked chicken, broccoli, and ramen. With a bottle of Indian curry sauce, all you need do is add rice and some cooked chicken for a wonderfully spicy meal.

- You can make lots of great pasta salads with ramen—which has the bonus of being dirt cheap. Just add some chopped up, cooked vegetables and a little bit of your favorite cooked meat and some kind of sauce. Just don't use their too-salty seasoning sauce.

- You can do similar things with a box of dirt-cheap macaroni and cheese. Add little bits of meat and/or vegetable for a cheap, quick meal that kids love.

- Progresso and Campbell's Chunky are the best canned soups for eating (as opposed to cooking). Some of the Lipton Kettle Creation varieties of dried beans and vegetables, combined with meat and water, produce some hearty soups almost as tasty as the Fantastic Foods soup lunch cups. Buy an interesting loaf of bread at the supermarket bakery and you've got a meal.

- Try some of those frozen vegetable-and-sauce mixes made by Pillsbury (called Create a Meal!) and Birds Eye (called Easy Recipe). All you need to add is some meat and/or pasta or rice to make a main meal. Families will want to try these to see which, if any, varieties they like. Frozen stir fry vegetable mixes are also good for making a quick meal out of some leftover chicken. Just add some Oriental sauce.

- Dessert ideas: You can't go wrong with a box of Pepperidge Farm or Carr cookies with or without premium ice cream. (Hint: You can buy Pepperidge Farm products at good prices at their company outlet stores.) A good ice cream served with fresh fruit or a liqueur also makes an extremely easy but delicious dessert. Breyers Vienetta ice cream cakes are delicious and elegant (if not cheap), and are as easy to make as taking them out of your freezer. In my opinion, says Wyman, Duncan Hines makes the best quality cake and brownie mixes.

- Breakfast ideas: Sara Lee coffee cake, or use those coupons Dunkin' Donuts is always giving out and buy a dozen muffins for the price of six.

- Kid ideas: Make up for your lack of culinary skill with fun ideas like serving breakfast (eggs, pancakes, and so forth) for dinner and making everyone say "Good Morning" and talk about the day as if it was just beginning. The kids will love it.

After reading Wyman's suggestions, you might think you could happily spend the rest of your life at Level Three or lower. But eventually you are likely to hanker for something a bit more challenging, something made from scratch, if you will. The next two levels are both homemade meals: Think of them as Easy Scratch and Hard Scratch. Let's start with the former.

Level Four

These are easy, homemade meals that require just a smidgen more of cooking effort. The world is full of great cookbooks that provide step-by-step directions that simplify things for even the most neophyte of cooks. Several good books you might want to check out are:

- *Dad's Own Cookbook,* by Bob Sloan. This is a good basic cookbook written by a guy for other guys. It features simple, doable recipes, and includes a great section on food preparation for parties.

- *Where is Mom Now that I Need Her?* by Kent and Betty Rae Fradsen. A basic survival guide for men marooned alone in the kitchen.

- *The 5 in 10 Cookbook—5 Ingredients in 10 Minutes or Less,* by Paula Hamilton. Hamilton, a food writer and home economist married to a chef, recently explained in a newspaper interview that despite her family's culinary background, both she and her husband are often too busy to cook. "Mealtime had become a disaster," she said. "What became clear was that we desperately needed some new cooking strategies." The result of her efforts is 164 delectable recipes like "butterflied steaks with sun-dried tomatoes and mushrooms" which takes less time than ordering pizza—recipes one food critic called "exquisite."

- *20 Minute Meals,* by Marian Burros—a great compendium of fast, easy, and healthy options.

- *60 Minute Gourmet* and *More 60 Minute Gourmet,* by Pierre Franey— for those who don't mind taking a little extra time to prepare great cuisine.

Toys for Boys

Another Level Four option that appeals to many guys depends on gadgetry. I learned this past Mother's Day that women generally do not like gifts that can be plugged in. Actually, what I did was *relearn* this lesson for myself. When I was a kid, my father gave my mother a waffle iron one Christmas, a gift that quickly entered the family lore as perhaps the least wanted present in the history of our clan. Such memories, of course, were far from my thoughts when I selected what I considered to be the perfect Mother's Day present for Debbie: a top-of-the-line, rechargeable Dustbuster Deluxe. The gizmo remained in our house only seconds after the wrapping was removed—then Debbie was off to the return counter.

We men, on the other hand, like anything that runs on electricity (and if it can be operated by remote control or contains microchips, it's even better). "I'm really into cooking gadgets," explains Henry, a forty-five-year-old businessman who handles 75 percent of his family's cooking. "I have a pasta maker, a Crock-Pot, a Cuisinart, a rice steamer, a convection oven, a coffee bean grinder, and an espresso machine—all sorts of fun things that make cooking more 'modular' and easier to clean up."

Henry's not alone in his embrace of gizmos. A couple years ago, before they became widespread, my friend Mike ordered a computerized breadmaker from a catalog. When it arrived, his wife had no idea how to use the thing and actually felt a bit intimidated by it. After looking at the rather daunting user's manual, she announced that she herself would never use this contraption—and she added that, in her opinion, microchips have no place in the kitchen. She predicted Mike's breadmaker would end up in the attic within two weeks.

It didn't, of course. Instead, Mike uses it three or four times every week to prepare a delicious assortment of homemade breads and pizza dough. His kids love it; so does his wife, who now admits that perhaps the microchip has a place in the kitchen after all.

I was so impressed with this that I asked Debbie to buy me a computerized bread maker for Christmas this year . I have been making delicious, hot bread for our family ever since. The model she bought me even comes with a timer—I put the flour, yeast, and so forth in at night, and set it to be done right when we wake up for breakfast. Add some honey or raspberry jam, and it's a great way to wake up.

High tech aside, perhaps the best way for men who aren't accustomed to cooking can learn to feel comfortable at Level Four is to do what Brian suggested at the beginning of this chapter: Ask a buddy who knows how to cook to give you a lesson.

Level Five

Okay, so you've had a few lessons from a friend, you can cook some great basics that your family actually likes, and your house is still standing, no victim to a kitchen fire. Maybe you've even purchased a little spiral notebook for notes—and started compiling your own "favorite recipes" cookbook. Maybe you've even started to think of cooking as fun and stress reducing. You put on a little music, take a nip of the cooking sherry, and lose yourself in a world of warmth and aroma.

At this point, you may just be ready for the Black Belt of cooking. I got the idea for Level Five during a fit of nostalgia two Christmases ago. Each Yuletide of my childhood, my mother prepared for our family a feast of roast beef and Yorkshire pudding—capped off with lemon meringue pie. My mother passed away four years ago, and I found myself asking Debbie to re-create this meal for me. She said she would—but that the meal might have more meaning for me if I learned how to make it. Of course, she was right.

Most of the recipes my mother had used were in the *Joy of Cooking*, a cookbook that's probably as close as any book comes to being indispensable. But as for the lemon meringue pie, I soon learned from my sister, our mother had coaxed the recipe out of an old friend, but she'd never written it down. To get this recipe for myself, I went to see my mother's friend, now in her eighties. During the course of our conversation, this woman told me some great stories about my mother that I'd never heard before.

I also learned how to make one other extravagant dinner that has great personal meaning for me. Shortly after Debbie and I were married, we went to Mexico for a three-month stay. A restaurant in the little town where we stayed made this delicious shrimp dish with garlic, dried peppers, and lime juice. On the night before we left to come back to the United States, I asked the cook—in my horribly broken Spanish—if she would share the recipe with us.

She wrote it down in Spanish, and, after a few translation difficulties, I finally figured out how to make the dish. We have *camerones con ajo* once or twice a year now, oftentimes pulling out our old Mexico photos to relive our honeymoon.

In the end, what makes a Level Five dish so good is not just the technical challenge, but the fact that the food has meaning above and beyond its delicious taste. A Level Five dish exists in the intersection of nutrients and spirituality; it is definitely something to pass on to your sons and daughters.

I can't, of course, give you a recipe for your Level Five meals—it's a quest each person must take on his or her own. One final thought, though. Once you've mastered your extravaganza, you might want to take a few minutes to jot down not only the recipes involved but the story behind the meal, that is, why exactly this wonderful collection of foodstuffs has such meaning for you. One day, you can bequeath these notes to your own sons and daughters—and the good times, as they say in New Orleans, can roll on in perpetuity.

Chapter 9

KEEP ON KEEPING ON

A Word of Encouragement and Hope for Harmony

Set thine house in order.
> —the Bible

I got in a fight one time with a really big guy, and he said, "I'm going to mop the floor with your face." I said, "You'll be sorry." He said, "Oh, yeah? Why?" I said, "Well, you won't be able to get into the corners very well."
> —Emo Phillips

I once audited a pension fund for laundry workers in California. It was a dying business, and the workers knew it. Now I ask myself, Why should I do my own laundry? Ruining my time off just to put these people out of work? It seems downright evil. Having a moral argument for getting out of a chore is the most liberating approach I have come up with yet. I have also told my wife that if I do the cleaning, I can't be held responsible for anything that happens to it. Between the moral argument and the threat of actually doing it, I haven't done laundry since we had Sears deliver the big washer and dryer. To this day, my wife still lets me get away with it. If she saw another man, I would try to understand what drove her to it; if she wanted to move to another town, I would consider her wishes; but if she made me do laundry, I wouldn't know how to deal with it. For that understanding, I love my wife.
> —Joe V.

It's late on a Sunday afternoon in February, and our home is scary. For the past two days, snow has kept us all housebound. Our boys, now three and seven, have tried to combat cabin fever by taking out and briefly playing with every toy, board game, puzzle, bristle block, and Lego they've ever owned.

When, after a few minutes, this grows old, they begin making forts throughout the house, stretching quilts, sheets, and sleeping bags from one chair to the next, stabilizing these with piles of pillows, books, sports trophies, and at least one precariously perched Victorian ottoman. The whole downstairs soon resembles a shanty town erected on a foundation of well-tamped dirt. The Sunday newspaper, with its profusion of ads and circulars, has itself taken wing like a flock of cranes eager to light on every flat surface the pages can find.

In the kitchen, unwashed dishes pile up in the sink, and garbage erupts from the trash can like a river of lava. In the dining room, Debbie, dazed, leafs through a stack of Metropolitan Homes *and* House Beautifuls, *scissoring out impossible layouts depicting worlds in which the likes of us will never dwell. But no sooner has she cut out an arts-and-crafts bungalow, or a European modern bathroom, than it slips from her hand and falls away to join the pizza boxes, dirty socks, Kleenexes, muddy boots, and Colonel Mustard game cards that now constitute the linoleum of our house.*

Every once in a while, one of the kids' electronic toys randomly emits a preprogrammed message. "Raptors escaping, Sector Three!"

For my part, I am just finished fingering the word Fraud *into the dust on the dining room table when the doorbell rings. As I move to answer it, everything seems to proceed in slow motion. I tunnel my way through the boys' shanty town—How far can the door be? All around me, I hear the growls of dinosaurs escaping the Jurassic Park compound. It seems to take me forever to reach the door, and my heart is pounding with fatigue and anxiety. Finally, I throw open the front door and am temporarily blinded by strobe lighting.*

"Hi," says a kindly but skeptical voice emanating from somewhere behind the blinding light. "I'm Oprah Winfrey. I understand you've written a book about chore wars. May we come in?"

In the several years it's taken me to plan, research, and write this book, I've endured more than one bout with this nightmare. *How dare you,* I chide myself, *have the gall to offer advice to others when your own house-hold is hardly a showcase of the home economical science?*

Surely my identical twin brother, whose home really is neat and clean, will waste no time ratting on me to Oprah, Jenny Jones, Montel, and anyone else who might want to boost ratings by exposing a hypocrite.

Never mind that our house rarely descends to the nightmare state. Never mind, as well, that when it does, our sons have a blast. And afterward, when the four of us have all pitched in to restore order to the place, the tremendous satisfaction we feel is turbocharged by the contrast with the chaos we've (at least for now) eliminated.

The truth is, for our family, a certain degree of messiness is not only tolerable but desirable—it is, in a very real way, the magic ingredient that differentiates a home from a museum or antiseptic magazine spread. A household that's never been draped with wall-to-wall tents, one that's never been overflowing with a glorious profusion of *stuff,* is just not a living home.

Or, to put it another way, when Debbie and I grow old, which photograph from our youth will bring us more smiles? One that shows our living room looking impeccable, not a pillow out of place, or the same room converted, by our sons' energy and ingenuity, into a kingdom of tents and dinosaurs?

I know the truth of this, of course, but that still hasn't stopped me from occasionally beating myself up over the less-than-perfect house-keeping we do. Just last week, when our son Ben brought home a shopping bag's worth of art projects he'd accumulated at school, the glue-and-sparkle-coated *oeuvres* quickly began to overflow throughout the whole downstairs.

It's amazing how fast this process happens, and how infectious it is. Pretty soon, Debbie and I found ourselves joining in—tossing junk mail on assorted end tables and desks, leaving newspapers to pile up unfolded wherever they happened to last be read, littering the kitchen countertops with bottles, cans, and microwave food boxes because there are just too many coats and boots on the floor to make it navigable to the kitchen trash and recycling bins.

Standing in the midst of all this, I suddenly felt a twinge of hopelessness, like a sailor trying to bail the *Titanic* with a small pail. In this moment, it hit me: This is what so many women feel in their bones, that they will be forever judged by the state of their home, that the vigilance and toil required to keep things right will be never-ending.

And as quickly as I realized that the chore wars are a problem that may never be entirely *solved,* so too did I realize that some significant détente can be reached, that this, in and of itself, is a kind of victory. I thought of all the couples who had graciously shared their own struggles with me, couples who slowly, in fits and starts, were making things better and fairer between them.

Couples like the Bulsecos, Donna and Dana, who started out bipolar and eventually grew into harmony. As Donna described this evolutionary process: "When Dana and I first got together, I couldn't understand how anyone could let such mess pile up. If the bathroom mirror was dirty, it would infuriate me. If the bed was left unmade, I'd hate to get in it at night. Gender was not an issue, except for the fact that I felt that it fell upon me, as a woman, to set the standards for cleanliness. It was left to Dana, as the man, to be as oblivious of the mess as possible. Housework became our main arena of conflict, and it caused us both a lot of unhappiness.

"Until one day, Dana sat me down and gave a little speech: 'If I'm willing to do more around the house, you have to be willing to live with how much I do, not criticize me to do more. If I move closer in spirit to your idea of clean, you, too, have to accommodate my idea of clean—which may not be as clean as yours.'

"All of a sudden, I realized that I had become a tyrant.

"I also realized that I really didn't subscribe to my mother's notions of cleanliness—that I'd always felt that the neatness she imposed was oppressive. I learned to enjoy clutter on the coffee table and only be fastidious about the kitchen (the cockroach dilemma!).

"Today, Dana and I are virtually the same in our chore sensibility. There are times we choose to just let everything pile up (although our young son Roy's stuff tends to make it impossible to walk through the house unless we pick it up), and we both have times when we tear through the house on a cleaning spree. But the endless conflicts that once made us both so unhappy now seem so long ago."

All around the nation, working men and women committed to each other are reaching similar accords. The peace may not be always perfect, and occasional backsliding to old mindsets is probably inevitable for both genders.

But by and large, such couples have proven that it is more than just theoretically possible to find balance and peace on the homefront. If chore wars are still tainting your home with sadness and anger, take heart from the example of so many others once similarly afflicted: You can make things better.

I wish you godspeed on the road to armistice.

INDEX

A

Adversaries to teammates, 113, 124

Aerobic capacity, 40, 170

American Association for Marriage and Family Therapy (AAMFT), 5–7, 9, 11–12, 14, 39, 54, 73–74, 113, 114, 120, 136

Anthropology, 10, 75, 142

Anxiety, chores as a way to reduce, 39, 61, 166, 196

Authority, giving up, 56, 92, 102, 134

Autocracy, the self-defeating nature of , 72

B

Barnett, Rosalind C., Ph.D., 10

Basket weaving vs. house building, 142, 146, 167

Benefits of chores, romantic and emotional, 40–41

Breadmakers, computerized, 189

Brohaugh, Nolan, M.S.W., 20, 58–59, 63–66, 74–75

C

Caretaker role, importance of, 57, 59, 66

Checklist: the lessons of therapy, 103

Children and chores, tips for getting help for, 143, 145–148

Children, disciplinary problems, 62

Chore Wheel, 132, 134

Chore Wars poll, DeVito vs. Redford, 28

Chore Wars test, who does more?, 45

Cleaning lessons, 167

Cleaning
  how to stop the dirt invasion, 173
  reducing the need to, 174
  the right tools, 175
  attack strategies, 176

Communal living, 129

Communication, 68, 89, 104, 110–111, 128–129, 131, 148, 153–154

G

Gay households, 14, 92
gender, 5, 11, 20, 34, 54, 61, 63–64, 99, 122, 140, 142, 196
Gender role(s) and differences, 5, 20, 54, 61, 63–64, 142
gender stereotypes, removing, 114
Generational change, 75

H

Hartman, Gail, M.A., 20, 38, 73–74, 93, 97–103
Hochschild, Arlie, 6, 12, 54, 73
House rules, 130
House meetings, 156–158
Housemate situations: special concerns, 129
Housemate horror stories, 15–18
Housesharing, 129

I

In-laws, 25, 52
Incompetence, male fear of, 20, 56, 65, 125
Intervention with roommate, 133

L

Lasswell, Marcia, 113–115, 120–122, 124–126, 128
Laundry, tips on, 177
Lesbians, 14
Letter of the law, 95–96, 105, 116
Low control vs. high control tasks, 123

M

Maid, 21, 92, 94, 131–132, 135, 144, 152, 160, 163–164, 173
Marital arguments, the effect on male and female job performance, 22, 62, 64, 70, 81, 108
Marriage, 1, 3, 5–6, 12, 14, 18, 35–36, 51, 55, 57, 62, 65, 74–76, 79, 81–82, 84–86, 88, 90–94, 97, 99–100, 103, 114, 127, 136, 139–140, 163, 173
Marshall, Nancy, Ed.D., 40, 62–64, 75
Master list and the art of compromise, 119, 121–122, 125, 183
Mathematical equality in chores, 38, 123
Mixed messages, 10, 104, 115
Month-by-month lease, importance of, 132
Multiple roles, the psychological rewards of, 40

S

Type-A personality, 39
Tyranny, 114, 198

U
Unemployment, 66

V
Valenzi, Margaret, 75, 164–165, 167–172
Van Leeuwen, Mary Stewart, 142

W
Weiner-Davis, Michele, M.S.W., 110–113
What Is a Life Worth?, 8
Women's work vs. men's work, 64, 78, 142
Wyman, Carolyn, 185

The *Chore Wars*
Nightmare Household Contest!

Attention Readers! We want to hear about your Chore Wars! Write to us before January 1, 1998, with your "wretched roommate" or "slothful spouse" story. The winner will receive a Chore Wars-style domestic reengineering from author and expert James Thornton, and we will provide a professional house cleaning!

 Send your story to:

Chore Wars Contest
2550 Ninth Street, Suite 101
Berkeley, CA 94710-2551
e-mail: Conaripub@aol.com

Conari Press, established in 1987, publishes books on topics ranging from spirituality and women's history to sexuality and personal growth. Our main goal is to publish quality books that will make a difference in people's lives—both how we feel about ourselves and how we relate to one another.

Our readers are our most important resource, and we value your input, suggestions, and ideas. We'd love to hear from you—after all, we are publishing books for you!

For a complete catalog or to get on our mailing list, please contact us at:

CONARI PRESS
2550 Ninth Street, Suite 101
Berkeley, California 94710-2551
800-685-9595 • Fax 510-649-7190 • e-mail Conaripub@aol.com